Cajun Zombie Chronicles:
Book Three

# THE
# KINGDOM
# DEAD

by

S. L. Smith

HOLY WATER BOOKS

Cajun Zombie Chronicles: Book Three
The Kingdom Dead

ISBN-13: 978-1-950782-32-1 (Holy Water Books)

HOLY WATER BOOKS
*At the unexpected horizons of the New Evangelization*

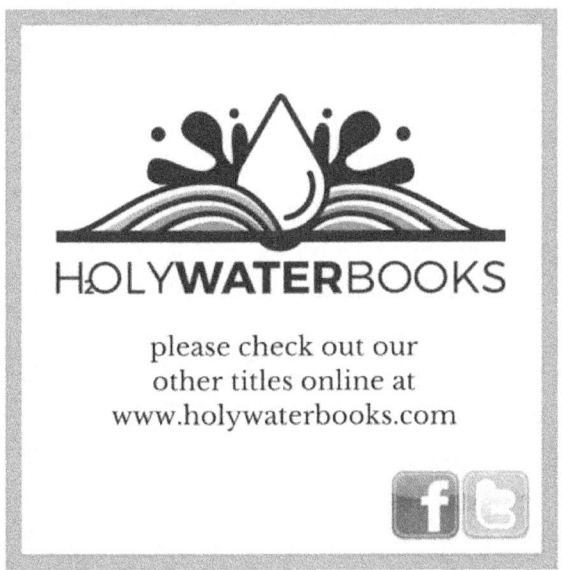

please check out our
other titles online at
www.holywaterbooks.com

Cover design by Holy Water Books

Cajun Zombie Chronicles: Book Three
# THE KINGDOM DEAD

## Table of Contents

# CHAPTER ONE: SMITHFIELD

Isherwood passed the binoculars to Justin, who soon thereafter passed them to Padre. They were lying beneath the crest of the levee, looking south along the River Road. Stretching out before them was one of the only straightaways on what was otherwise a tightly curving road. The only significant obstruction along the southern horizon, besides the levee itself, was a large home. It wasn't a plantation-style home, which were so common along the Mississippi River, though it was a plantation. Its gabled roofs, turret, and elaborate façade betrayed its Queen Anne, Eastlake style. At three stories, it towered over the landscape, rising high above the levee. It would have occupied an entire city block, if it wasn't it the middle of nowhere. It was something of an oddity along the river, but would prove too great a temptation, Isherwood was betting, for a band of survivors traveling on foot from Baton Rouge.

The survivors at St. Mary's had just returned from a rescue mission to Whiskey Bay to save the family of Isherwood's wife, when their radio operator received two urgent distress calls. The first was from their outpost in Livonia, which was experiencing increased zombie activity. This was likely the fault of the rescue mission, whose movements had likely drawn the immense Interstate 10 swarm northward to Livonia. The second transmission was from, allegedly, a small group of survivors who had recently escaped Baton Rouge across the "Old Bridge." This group was headed to St. Mary's and appeared to offer no ill will, though Isherwood was taking no chances.

For the most part, Isherwood's band of survivors had encountered only friendly and trustworthy groups of other survivors with a few notable exceptions. One band of religious fanatics had actually kidnapped Isherwood's child for God knew what purpose. It had been a church group with whom Aunt Tad and Uncle Jerry had once associated. Tad had resolved that situation quickly and ruthlessly. Nevertheless, Isherwood had decided to approach new bands of survivors from a posture of "trust, but verify."

Isherwood had only brought Justin and Father Simeon, called Padre, to intercept the survivors. He didn't want to leave St. Mary's unprotected, so they would also take responsibility for relieving the siege of Livonia, as well. They had left Patrick in charge of defending their home. After their rescue, Isherwood had left his in-laws at St. Mary's, where they would be nursed back to health by Aunt Tad and the others. He was counting on his father and brothers-in-law to recover quickly from the long-term effects of starvation. He knew their fledgling community really needed their help. Besides helping with their nascent attempts at ranching and farming, they could radically alter their ability to reach out and rescue other survivors and connect with other areas.

Isherwood hoped to intercept the survivors along River Road and, if they were friendly, enlist their help with Livonia. This would be a test of sorts, he thought. They had no way of knowing where the "Old Bridge" group was or how far they had come from the bridge, but Isherwood knew that the River Road was the only other route to St. Mary's besides the path that ran through Livonia. It was getting dark, too. If Isherwood was right, the survivors would likely shelter for the night at Smithfield.

Isherwood had wanted to observe the other group from afar and to listen in on their conversations while they still thought they were alone. But he was wrestling with his decision to lie exposed atop the levee. If he was so confident that the other group was going to stop at Smithfield, why hadn't he just waited for them inside the house. It would have been much easier to defend themselves inside the house, than out. Or, if a patch of the river dead came upon them from behind, they would be forced to flee down the levee, anyway. Isherwood tried forcing these thoughts from his head. He was having to do that a lot these days. It was too late to change now, anyway, he told himself.

Justin let himself slip down the levee apiece. "So what happens," he whispered.

"Keep your voice down, Justin." Isherwood scolded.

Padre and Justin exchanged glances. They would continue to cut their friend slack, but Isherwood seemed to be getting edgier and edgier.

"So what happens," Justin whispered again, and then thought better of it. "Ish, let's do this. If they don't come in the next half hour, I'll split off and scout the alternate routes on my own. We've got the radios. It's not like we'd be out of touch. *Much.*"

"We've been through *this.*" Isherwood said, his own voice rising above a whisper. "We're already too small a group. If these guys attack us, we're probably screwed as it is."

"Right." Justin pressed. "We're screwed either way if they're hostile. So let's just —"

"Shut it." Padre said suddenly. "They're here."

They all grew suddenly quiet and still. It took a while for Justin and Isherwood to see the figures emerge from the evening half-light, as Padre was still using the larger set of military-grade M830r binoculars. They both pulled out smaller, pocket-sized binoculars from their vests. They were walking in wedge formation down the center of River Road.

Padre was already scanning the side of the levee and the far side of the road for other flanking groups. "It's just the one group, I think. No more," he said. "Eight total. Well-armed."

"Women, children, elderly?" Isherwood asked.

Padre was about to respond, when Justin interrupted. "Is that a wheelchair?"

"It is," Padre answered. "An old woman, I think."

"They pass the first test," Isherwood answered. "But it could still be trap."

"Seriously?" Justin winced, but Isherwood didn't respond.

"Anything tailing them?" Isherwood asked Padre.

"Nothing yet." Padre answered.

As they watched, the group slipped quickly off the roadway. The sun had slipped below the horizon and it was beginning to grow dark quickly. Two of them broke off from the back of the group and jogged around either side of the large house. They were moving with precision. Isherwood and his group didn't see these two come back from behind the house, and they assumed they entered the house from the back door.

Another pair of people proceeded up the front steps of the house. The last four, including the women in the wheelchair and the person who was pushing her, remained on the front lawn about fifteen feet from the front steps. They scanned the surrounding area while the others cleared the house.

The work of scanning the house was done quickly and quietly from what Isherwood and the others could tell. The second pair scanned and cleared the porch which wrapped around the front part of the house and then returned to the front doors. They opened the doors quietly without needing to knock them in noisily. Thereafter, from the levee, they saw only one muzzle flash from inside the dark house, but heard no report. "These guys are impressive," Justin mused. "Got silencers, too. Wonder why they're coming to *us*?"

Men appeared from inside the house to give the all clear sign to those still waiting on the front lawn. The one man pushed the wheelchair to the front steps and then moved to the front of the wheelchair and knelt down. The old woman rose from the chair and climbed onto the kneeling man's back. He hurried up the stairs with the old woman clinging to his back, as if he had done it many times before. Another one collapsed the wheelchair and carried it up the stairs separately.

"Kinda touching, actually," Justin said with mocking sweetness.

Padre nodded. "I sure hope these are good guys."

In another couple minutes, the lawn was empty and the house was again quiet. If it weren't for a small glint of light from inside, the place would look entirely abandoned.

Isherwood tapped his buddies on the shoulder, and the three of them slid down below the crest of the levee. "Look, Ish – I don't see any way we can get close enough to the house to listen in without being noticed. Maybe we just ought to do the neighborly thing?"

"What's that? Bring over a Jell-O mold?" Isherwood grumbled in disdain.

"Hey," Justin said with irritation. "That's *my* line."

A flash appeared in the shadow of the levee. It was Isherwood's smile. "Yeah, you know, I'm feeling alright about these guys."

Padre nodded, though the others couldn't tell. "Me, too. Besides, I don't think sneaking up on these guys would be too wise."

"Agreed," Isherwood said. "Only, you stay back. Okay, Padre? If we don't give you the all clear sign after a half hour, you do what you think best."

"I'll keep my radio on, so you can listen in," Justin added.

"Good," Isherwood agreed. "You ready, Justin?"

"Just me and my AR, is all." He said, tapping his trusty gun and giving it a little kiss.

"Great," Isherwood said, shaking his head. "Padre, would you give us your blessing, please?"

*****

A minute later, Isherwood and Justin were standing in the front lawn of Smithfield. The stairs rose before them to a height well over their heads. "God, this place is massive." Justin whispered.

"Would make a good outpost." Isherwood nodded. "Just have to remove these stairs, and it would be a castle."

Justin looked at him awkwardly, wondering why Isherwood was hesitating while they were out in the open. Isherwood caught Justin's look and turned away a little too quickly. "I just, uh," Isherwood started and then stopped.

"Ish?" Justin looked at him with an uncomfortable grin. "You're not about to tell me you love me, are you?"

Isherwood wrinkled his brow in frustration. He wasn't prepared for Justin's banter just now. "I just wanted to say sorry. I've been fraying a bit at the edges recently, and I don't mean to take it out on you."

Justin just stared back at him stupidly. "Ah, hell." Isherwood burst out, louder than he should have. "Forget it. Nevermind. Forget I said …"

Justin cracked a smile. "Dude, don't be an idiot. You got nothing to apologize for. You understand. I owe you – we all owe you – big time. Besides, if you don't let off a little steam every once in a while, you'll pop: eyeballs, entrails, snot – everywhere. It's cool, okay?"

"Thanks, buddy," Isherwood said. "Now, let's shut up and do this thing." Together, they began walking up the stairs. They weren't trying to be stealth. The last thing they wanted was to surprise the new occupants of Smithfield. Even if they had wanted to be stealth, it would have been impossible on these stairs. They might as well be setting off firecrackers for all the creaking of the old boards. Isherwood wondered to himself how the other group had climbed these stairs so quietly before, especially the one who had carried the old woman on his back. They should have heard the same cacophony all the way to the levee.

Isherwood stopped at the top of the stairs and leaned over, reaching for the floor of the porch. He knocked twice and then twice again. It wasn't loud enough to draw zombies, he hoped. It was hopefully enough, however, to alert the occupants to their *living* presence. Isherwood and Justin stood still at the top of the stairs for a minute or so, and then Isherwood tried knocking again.

"*Shh*, man," a voice suddenly interrupted Isherwood mid-knock. "They're not far behind us. You'll send them right to the friggin' doorstep."

Isherwood jerked his head up in surprise. He wasn't expecting such instant familiarity between the groups.

They couldn't see who was speaking, but they now saw that the one of the tall front doors had been cracked open. "Get *in*! Quick! Before they see you."

Isherwood and Justin followed the instructions of the disembodied voice blindly. Before Isherwood disappeared inside the house, he turned back to the levee and gave Padre a sign to alert him to the oncoming hoard. Isherwood pointed at his eyes, then down the River Road, then made a 'Z' with his left hand. Somebody, Isherwood thought it might've been Aunt Tad, had remembered how a 'Z' was made in sign language. A 'Z' was just swished out in the air, like Zorro did with his whip.

A middle-aged man rushed Isherwood and Justin inside the doors and quickly turned his attention back to the front door. He took great pains to turn the doorknob slowly, so as not to make a sound. Then, he returned a doorstop to its place that braced both doors closed. Justin thought he had remembered seeing something a similar door brace on an infomercial – back when there were infomercials – advertised alongside the "Help! I've fallen and I can't get up" necklace monitor.

"Good God, man," Isherwood whispered. "That must be some kind of swarm you got on your tail."

The man still hadn't turned to face them. He was leaning forward to stare past the thick curtains that covered the beveled glass insets of the door. "Yeah, we used to be *three* times this many," the man admitted somberly.

"You, uh," the man began, finally turning to face them. He looked haggard and clearly had not seen a razor in some time. He looked frenzied, like a man who had been on the run for days. "You signaled to somebody out there, didn't you?"

"I did," Isherwood admitted. "I'm …"

"I'm sorry about that," the haggard man interrupted. "He's probably dead already. There's nothing we can do for him now."

"What d'you mean?" Justin asked in a hush.

"*Shh*," the haggard man insisted. "Not so loud."

"What d'you mean?" Justin repeated a few decibels softer. "I still don't see anything out there."

"It's okay, though," Isherwood added, matching their hushed tones. "Padre can take care of himself."

"Padre? Did you say 'Padre'?" The haggard man asked suddenly. His eyes grew wide and he hurriedly turned back to the doorknob.

Isherwood lunged for the man's hands. "No, no. It's okay, really. He's more than able to ..."

"But he's a priest, isn't he?" The haggard man said as he forced his muscles to relax beneath Isherwood's grip.

"Yeah, actually," Justin said. "How'd you know?"

The haggard man was shaking his head in disbelief. "It's why we've come, that's why. The old woman, she – well, she'll have to explain it to you."

"God," he said, turning back to the door and trying to shove his eyeball past the curtain. "You sure he'll be okay."

"Yeah, yeah," Isherwood tried comforting the man. "He's been through and survived much worse already."

"Dang," Justin said as he thought aloud. "Y'all seemed to be so much more confident when we were watching you."

"Did we?" The man asked, grinning despite himself. "Yeah, I suppose we're pretty practiced by now. It took us *weeks* to get out of Baton Rouge, and we only started downtown, not far from the Old Bridge." The 'Old Bridge' was what the locals called the older of the two Mississippi River Bridges. There were actually three Mississippi River bridges in the area now. Construction finished on the Audubon Bridge just a few years ago. About a month ago, Isherwood had blocked off the Audubon Bridge in an effort to make an island out of St. Maryville, cutting off as many routes as he could into the small town. The job was nearly completed, as the town was surrounded by moats of water between False River and the Mississippi River. Before blocking the bridge, Isherwood had led a slow train of zombies over it, like the Pied Piper of Hamlin. He had cleared out maybe three thousand of the five thousand plus zombies staggering around St. Maryville. Even with this success, however, St. Maryville had still been harried by legions of the so-called River Dead. The Mississippi River would periodically belch up swarms of zombies carried by its currents from parts unknown. Isherwood, however, had plans for these water-borne swarms.

"But you seem so on edge for someone with that kind of experience," Justin continued.

"You would, too," Isherwood scolded. "If *you* hadn't had a decent night's sleep in weeks."

The man looked back at them. His eyes were wide as though only vaguely aware of their presence. He might have been talking to himself. "'A good night's sleep'?

Don't even know what that means anymore." He swung his head back at them and smiled. "I'm Chet, by the way." He pushed his hand towards them indicating a handshake, but retrieved it before either Isherwood or Justin could respond.

Chet was back again looking through the narrow opening between the curtain and the door. He moved quickly to the next room, a parlor. He crept around to the side of a larger window. There was a knick-knack table full of small animal figurines between him and the window. One wrong move and there would be a cascade of ceramics tumbling to the floor. He edged around the table without so much as wobble.

Chet stood by the window for what seemed like an hour. Justin and Isherwood blinked when he finally turned back to them. Chet was already back in the foyer by the time they re-opened their eyes. He put his hands on their shoulders. "They're here," he whispered. Then, with a small push, he said, "Follow me."

He led them to a stairway at the back of the house. They'd just passed a perfectly good stairway by the front door, Justin thought to himself. He assumed Chet was taking them this way to muffle, if not avoid, the symphony of creaking steps. Justin wasn't sure if we wanted to be going up in this house while a swarm surrounded it, but he acquiesced for now. *Better than this movie ending in the basement,* he thought to himself darkly, remembering how the people had trapped themselves in the original *Night of the Living Dead*. His thoughts began to wander from there. *Or, was that the remake?* He asked himself.

There was a small splash of light at the top of the stairs. There was a figure waiting for them in the shadows. Isherwood and Justin saw that he was another scruffy-bearded man, as they passed him. He watched the pair ominously as they passed by. Beyond the top of the stairs, the space quickly broadened into another parlor. The parlor sat in the middle of the house as sort of a meeting place and lounge between several bedrooms. They were few windows, and none that looked out the front of the house. The parlor was well situated after all, Justin observed, to weather the passing swarm.

Other than the guard at the top of the stairs, the rest of the group was resting and repacking their backs along the floors and pair of couches at the center of the room. They exchanged furtive glances with the newcomers. Between the two couches, there was a pair of armchairs. In one of these, the old woman was sitting. Her wheelchair was leaning against the wall behind her.

Justin started as he suddenly noticed movement above the old woman's chair. He looked up to see, he quickly realized, his own reflection staring back at him. There was a tall mirror hanging on the way, an old one by the look of it. The reflection had large sections of discoloration. He wondered for a moment at his changed appearance. He looked just like Chet and the other scruffy-bearded man. If they were all put in a line-up, he would be hard-pressed to pick out *himself*. He smiled briefly, despite himself, as he marveled at the weight he had lost. "Ain't no diet like a zombie apocalypse diet," he mumbled to himself.

"What's that?" Isherwood whispered beside him. Justin just shook his head when Isherwood turned to him for a response. He was glad no one could see him blushing in the dark room.

Chet led them to the old woman. "Miss Abby," he said. The others slowly gathered at and around the two couches. There was a single, thick candle burning on a low oval coffee table which stood between the couches and armchairs at the very center of the parlor. "These two men," Chet said, motioning to Isherwood and Justin. "These are, well, actually. I never got their names." Chet motioned for the men to come over and introduce themselves to the old woman. Another one of the men, not the one from the top of the stairway, stiffened as they approached the old woman, Isherwood noticed even in the dark. *I bet he's the one who carried her up the stairs.* Both he and the old woman were black, Isherwood also noticed. *Her grandson, maybe?* The old woman's face was illuminated in the flickering candlelight. Her face was creased with what seemed like a thousand wrinkles. *Maybe great-grandson*, Isherwood corrected himself.

"Isherwood," he said, introducing himself. He was leaning down to the old woman, as if bowing. She raised her hand to him at a slow, measured pace. He took her slender, well-weathered hand into both of his own. Her grip, Isherwood quickly noticed, was anything but feeble, betraying her overall appearance. Her eyes, deep set from age, glittered black like the carapaces of two searching beetles. They twinkled at the newcomers in the candlelight.

Justin introduced himself in a similar manner, and the wrinkles began gathering together at the center of her forehead, like curtains being slowly bunched together. "But where is the other one?" She whispered. "The priest? He was here. I know he was."

Chet answered before the others could respond. "Yes, Miss Abby," he said, as her eyes and head slowly moved in his direction. "He's still outside. They didn't know if we could be trusted, you see?" Isherwood felt suddenly sheepish at the idea. He realized dimly that, in just the passing moments, he can come to trust this group entirely. There was a certain, undeniable magnetism to the old woman, he thought to himself.

"He'll be alright," Isherwood found himself trying to reassure the old woman and the others. "He's very ..."

"Yes," the old woman interrupted. "He'll be jus' fine." Her head slowly sank back to her chest and her eyes returned to the candlelight. "And he will visit us in the morning."

As they watched, waiting for further explanation, the old woman's eyes slowly closed like those of the ancient sphinx, and she was asleep.

Isherwood and Justin looked around in confusion, feeling suddenly odd. They were still leaning in to listen to the old woman. Even now, just moments later, her ancient lips begin to puff rhythmically with the soft growls of snoring. They looked around in confusion, but the others seemed to be used to interactions like this. Chet was looking at them with a little grin curling the corner of his mouth.

They were soon, all of them, asleep, as if somehow all their sleep cycles were linked to the old woman's. This, despite the growing sound of hundreds of feet shuffling past the house.

# CHAPTER TWO:
# MORNING

There was a screw-top canister with a rubber seal in the kitchen filled with Morning Treat coffee. The group of eight along with Isherwood and Justin boiled water on the stove – the house likely had its own propane tank and some unknown portion of it remained filled – and poured it by hand through a Mr. Coffee electric-powered coffee pot.

Isherwood stood against the frame of the back door, looking out through the glass and the screen beyond. The rising cloud of steam from a raised coffee mug parted as it rose past his face. There was a small of pile of stacked corpses, the former residents of Smithfield that had been cleared out by the advance team. He looked from the pile to the pitted back lawn and its trampled grass.

"That swarm is headed right for our home," he announced to the rest of the crowded kitchen. There was a thick table at the center of the kitchen, which looked to be attached to the home and showed signs of wear to match. Miss Abby had been carried downstairs by the other man that Isherwood believed to be her grandson.

"What are you suggesting? We can't take them on ourselves," Chet answered him.

"They'd run right over us. Are you – you can't be *serious*?" A youngish woman asked. She was fair-skinned with a handful of freckles and a length of red hair pulled back in a ponytail.

Isherwood put a hand up in protest. "Look, all I said was they're headed straight for my *home*, you know, my wife and kids." He regretted mentioning his family almost immediately. It wasn't just that he had given away his weak point to these people, whom, except for Miss Abby, he still wasn't sure about. It was the dark clouds that seemed to pass over their faces when he made mention of his *still living* family.

"We've taken on larger before and with just the three of us," Justin added distractedly, as he rummaged through the various cabinets. He eventually popped up with an old box of Frosted Flakes, digging in eagerly. "We had more ammo back then, though."

"Plus, we've got Livonia to think about," Isherwood added. "That's one of our outposts," he added, explaining to the others. "We got a distress call from them before we left to intercept y'all. We were hoping," he added sheepishly, "that you might join us in helping them out."

"Say what?" said the man, who Isherwood thought might be Miss Abby's grandson.

"Yeah, buddy," said an older man with a black bandanna hanging loosely around his neck. He seemed to be sweating all the time. Isherwood guessed this had been one of the advance team that had scouted the house. "We ain't got much juice left before we flat-out collapse."

"Understood," Isherwood answered. "We do have *alternatives*," he said delicately.

"*Alternatives?*" The redhead repeated indignantly, balling her hands into fists.

"Hush, hush, *husshh*," Miss Abby breathed gently from the head of the table. "The priest already has all this worked out for us. He'll be stopping by any minute now."

Isherwood wrinkled his brow and turned his head instinctively to look out onto the back lawn, as if expecting to see Padre walking up. When he looked back to the kitchen, he felt that the tension had actually cleared. Justin was trying to give him a look, but he ignored him. It didn't matter. He knew exactly what Justin was thinking. The group of eight actually calmed down after listening to Miss Abby. It had been a strange sight, though. They had visibly relaxed.

"Dude," Justin said, sidling up to Isherwood and refusing to take his hint. "It's like she's got them bewitched or something," he whispered.

Isherwood just barely shook his head, hoping Justin would get the hint. He couldn't talk about it. Not right now. Miss Abby was actually looking at him. He didn't know if she could actually see him on the opposite side of the kitchen, but he was beginning to think she had something that made up for old age and poor eyesight.

*****

It was only a couple minutes when they heard a soft tapping. In hindsight, Miss Abby's words were eerily prophetic.

17

It was Padre. He had just walked straight up to the front door. It was Chet who first heard him knocking. He moved suddenly to the front door. The others noticed his absence almost immediately. They all fell into step behind Chet, except the old woman and her grandson. The others took up positions behind and to either side of Chet even before he reached the front door. Isherwood and Justin sort of ambled towards the others in curiosity. Looking around, Isherwood saw they were all suddenly armed. He hadn't noticed their weapons at the table, and all of a sudden they were locked and loaded. *I sure hope these guys are good guys,* he thought to himself, *'cause we need 'em.*

As if reading his thoughts, Justin turned to Isherwood and whispered, "Scary." His eyes widened in admiration.

Miss Abby gave the younger black man's arm a gentle squeeze. He turned to her, and she nodded to him. A moment later, Isherwood was surprised to see the wheelchair had been rolled to a spot in the front parlor directly behind him. He saw the old woman leaning in her chair to get a good look at the front door. He smiled at her, though she didn't notice, because she looked almost young again, like a school girl giddy with anticipation. Looking around, Isherwood could feel the house filling with anticipation. The redhead was again balling her free hand into a little first.

When Chet opened the door, the man standing at the door seemed almost comical compared to the anticipation that was awaiting him. It was Padre, exactly on cue. His cassock had been muddied by a night on the run, but otherwise he looked normal. He adjusted his glasses and nodded at them silently. As typical, he was a man of few words. He nevertheless struck an imposing figure with the rifles crossed against his back and the .44s holstered on either side. One of the pistols was covered in mud, and had for most of the night been given up for lost. All of it, except for the knives he kept inside the cassock, had been useless during the night.

"Come on in. Miss Abby's been expecting you," Chet finally said after taking a moment to scan the front lawn and the road beyond.

Padre looked over to Isherwood before moving. Isherwood nodded and wrinkled his brow a bit, as if to say, 'oh, yeah, definitely, nothing to worry about here.'

Padre nodded back and silently followed Chet's gesture of welcome into the foyer of the large house. "Well," Padre said, standing in their midst. Everybody was just staring at him. "How about some coffee?"

"Excellent plan," Isherwood said with a sly grin.

*****

"Wait, so you're Holly and *you're* Gill?" Padre was pointing at the two twenty-something women in the 'Group of Eight,' or so Isherwood had taken to calling them, what was left of them. They were doing a round of introductions at Padre's request, something Isherwood and Justin regretted not doing sooner.

"Yeah, I'm Gill, *Karen* Gill, actually," said the redhead, who was acting much less fiery now that Padre had come. "It's sort of a reference to a book," Gill was explaining and dismissing with a wave of her hand. "Nevermind."

"I get it," Isherwood smiled. "*Anne of Green Gables*, right? But it's ironic because you're red-headed, but called 'Gill' like Gilbert, but not 'Anne'."

"Yeah, something like that." The girl smiled, brushing loose strands of her hair back behind her ear. Isherwood couldn't tell if she was impressed or uncomfortable, so he quickly backed off.

"That's gonna be confusing," Justin said, returning to the introductions. "Because I'd expect Holly to have the red hair." After noticing a few confused expressions, he added with a shrug, "you know, like 'holly' berries?"

"It's Holland, actually." The somewhat younger girl corrected, pursing her lips. She wore oversized clear plastic glasses that reminded Isherwood of his mom's glasses growing up in the Eighties. She was somewhat big in the hips and wore jeans that seemed to accentuate, rather than diminish, this. "But, yeah, Holly is cool," she said dismissively, while tightening her grip on her cup of coffee and staring into its depths.

"And you're Miss Abby," Padre said changing the subject and pointing to the old woman.

"Wait," Chet interrupted. "How'd you know that? Did she say her name – did anybody?"

Miss Abby brushed him off with a wave. "Nevermind about that, dear. Mor'un one way to skin a cat." She and Padre exchanged conspiratorial glances. "I 'spect you're wondering why we've come all this way to see you and the other priest." Padre nodded in silent answer. "Because," the old woman said with severity. Her bottom teeth would've jutted out from beyond her bottom lip, if she still had any bottom teeth. "He's got somethin' that belongs to me. That's why."

"Something that belongs to you?" The younger black man asked. "We've come all this way for a *thing*?"

"And this young handsome thing is Hillman," Miss Abby continued, ignoring him while tapping the arm of the man Isherwood had assumed was her grandson. "My great-great-grandson, or something like that. He and I are all that's left of a once large family." Hillman nodded and gave his grandmother a meaningful look.

"Hill, actually. I just go by 'Hill.' Hillman is – *was* – my dad." His smile faltered as he said it. As he corrected himself, a dark cloud swept across his face. "And that guy over there," Hill said with a grin. "Calls himself 'Lee Majors.'"

"Like the 'Bionic Man'?" Isherwood said smiled suspiciously.

"'Six Million Dollar'," Lee corrected in a somewhat bored and officious tone. "Actually," he continued in sort of a droning, effeminate way, "It's Lee Mayers, but it's the Apocalypse and I was like 'what the hell?' People have been pointing out the similarity my whole dang life anyway. I'll file the appropriate paperwork as soon as the opportunity arises, how's that sound?" He laughed, hissing through his nose.

S. L. Smith

"And the guy at the end," Hill said, having fully regained his joking manner, "who looks nothing at all like a terrorist, is Jarrah."

There was an Arabic-looking man standing at the end of the table closest to where Isherwood was leaning against the kitchen counter. Isherwood was surprised to see the man. He figured that he must have just come in. He also noticed that the older man with the black bandanna was now gone. Isherwood guessed that the bandanna man had just relieved Jarrah of guard duty.

Jarrah laughed an easy laugh at Hill's banter. Isherwood figured it must be an ongoing joke between the two men. "Yes, and waiter?" Jarrah shot back at Hill with an effete smirk. "I'll take today's special along with a glass of whatever's open, sound good?"

"Sure thing," Hill said smiling and shaking his head. "Only today's special is nothin' with a side of kiss my ..."

"That's enough, dear," Miss Abby said, interrupting her great-great grandson just in time. Nevertheless, the whole kitchen filled with hushed laughter. "It's a good group we have here," the old woman continued as the laughter died down. "If a little too rowdy for my tastes."

"What about the man with the black bandanna?" Isherwood asked.

"Old, bald, and ugly, you mean?" Lee Majors asked. "That's Hoskins. 'Skins' for short."

"Well," Lee continued after a pause. "Miss Abby says you've got the plan, Father." Isherwood could tell it was not second nature for Lee to speak in respectful tones about anyone – he looked as though there was something bitter in his mouth – but he managed it for the old woman and the priest.

Padre nodded slowly and a short smile briefly emerged from his beard, as he peered down into his coffee mug. He then pushed the mug away and folded his hands in front of him, as he thought over what he was about to say. He almost let the moment slip away from him with an overlong pause. Lee was beginning to move his head as though he were about to speak, when Padre finally spoke up.

"The swarm passed us by and is still heading north to St. Maryville, as you all might've guessed. Sort of a disaster about to happen. Another swarm may be assailing Livonia, too. One choice is to go after this swarm first, a divide and conquer approach. Another would be to lead this one to Livonia so we could take care of both swarms at the same time and from behind cover. But," Padre paused for a second to adjust his glasses on his nose. "There may be another option. A *better* option."

Many of them leaned in closer at this. There was actually a twinkle in Isherwood's eye. Padre actually looked over to Isherwood and smiled, knowing the third option was always his favorite. *Here we go,* Isherwood thought to himself. *Plan 'C' for Plan Chicken.*

"We're just downriver from where the southern end of False River comes closest to reuniting with the Mississippi. This is also the last area we need to seal up to finish making St. Maryville an island. We can't afford to go amphibious like we did

20

before," Padre said looking directly at Isherwood and knowing what he was thinking. "Because the only amphibious spot where both swarms could be united, inside the lines, is in the southern bend of the lake. We can't just fill the lake up with zombies and not expect terrible consequences down the road once they start scrambling back up the banks, nipping at swimmers' toes, etc."

"So that's everything we can't do." Jarrah said, "what's left?"

"We have this way of using the zombies' bodies," he explained to the newcomers. "The bodies, once killed or re-killed or whatever, act as 'self-building barricades.' It's worked great for us, but it uses a lot of bullets. But that mounding of the corpses is what gave me the idea. You see, there's this factory …"

# CHAPTER THREE:

# THE FACTORY PLAN

"Y̶ou sure about this?" Karen Gill, who the newcomers just called "Gill," asked.

Padre was again looking through his binoculars and lying just below the crest of the levy. He had passed the bigger nautical binoculars on to Isherwood before the groups split up. He and a few others, including Gill, were staring into the field which stretched out in front of them for hundreds of acres. The field was ringed with trees made hazy by the distance.

"Doesn't much matter now," Padre whispered in response. He was watching the remnants of the northward-marching horde. The main bulk of it had already disappeared around the line of trees at the edge of the fields. Stragglers stretched backward from the main horde for another half mile or so, just forward of their position. "But yeah, the idea came like an idea should come, if it's coming from the right place."

Karen looked at him quizzically and almost contemptuously. She could see a smile creasing Padre's beard, and decided he was just mocking her. She could feel her hands again mashing into fists.

They had left Padre's Humvee on the River Road a mile back, so the sound of the engine wouldn't turn the swarm around prematurely. They didn't want the swarm to notice their arrival until the time was right. Padre kept peaking back at his watch, as the swarm gradually disappeared before them.

After another couple of minutes, Padre lowered the binoculars for the last time. Turning to the others, he cleared his throat to get their attention. "Okay," he whispered. "Let's get down the levy and across the fence before we start making noise, though." The others nodded their assent and soon their small group was trotting down the far side of the levy towards the road. Besides Padre and Gill, there was Holly and Lee Majors. Isherwood and Justin had left with the remaining newcomers, except for Miss Abby and Hill. These were to stay at Smithfield and make no noise while the horde was re-routed past the home by Padre and the others. Chet, Jarrah, and Hoskins had been sent with Isherwood and Justin. Each of these men had some degree of technical ability which might be used to enhance Padre's plan at the factory. Hoskins, they discovered soon into their planning, had actually worked at a similar type of factory. Padre had taken this as confirmation of his plan. Isherwood, too, had already offered several ideas to enhance Padre's original idea.

The four of them were soon standing on the warm surface of the asphalt road. "Alright, *now*. Go." Padre said, as he pointed a flare gun skyward. The flare streaked red and skittered through the air in a tall arc. When it finally burst above their hands, they felt suddenly the gaze of a thousand eyes turning slowly in their direction. They were utterly exposed. They were a feast of roadkill, just waiting to be devoured.

The others suddenly erupted in a delayed response to Padre's command. Lee Majors didn't need much encouragement, despite his outwardly, cynical demeanor. He started hollering like a madmen and shooting his pistol into the air like Yosemite Sam. He was also cursing a blue streak like the Looney Tune. He appeared to be using this opportunity to release his long-pent up rage. Holly huffed in discomfort at Lee's display of emotion. Padre, apparently ignoring the crazed man's language, placed one of his large hands across the man's shoulder to counsel him, "Don't waste the ammo, Lee." Then, pointing at a place just astride the road, Padre said, "use it."

It hadn't taken long. There were already three of four of the stragglers from the main group nearing them from the far side of the road. After dispatching the first zombie at a surprising distance for a pistol – over twenty yards – Lee had turned along with the women from his group to flee down the road.

"Wait," Padre said.

"Wait?" Gill asked indignantly. "Are you *nuts*?" Holly, as well, sighed in mock-agony.

Lee, instead of complaining, actually turned around at Padre's instructions and returned to his side. "Dumb Dora," he said, shaking his head and patting his forehead. "He's right. We can't leave until we see the main mass of those things come back around the corner."

The redhead was nodding in anger. Her lips were pursed so tight, it looked as though her whole body was about to be sucked through a straw into the vacuum of space. There was also a crazed look in her face that grew and then softened. "If that's how it's gonna be, fine." Gill grabbed Holly's hand, surprising the other girl out her teenage angst as she lurched forward. "Boys," she said, tipping an imaginary hat as she passed Padre and Lee dragging Holly behind her.

Gill left Holly teetering on the edge of the road, as she hopped across the deep ditch that ran alongside it. "Sure," Gill said. "Stay there, Holland. Pop their little heads if they come stumbling into the ditch. When Gill had first let go of the other girl's hand, Holly's face was a mess of emotions, mostly indignation. When Gill looked back, Holly's mood had clicked to an entirely new setting. She looked both resolute and sinister. A firmly rooted shadow, looming above the ditch with knives gleaming from either hand.

Padre was watching all this and nodding. "These two may be very helpful."

"Oh yeah, they're acid-blooded killing machines from hell when the mood takes them." Lee said matter-of-factly. "You wouldn't believe where we first came across them. They were threading their way through a helluva swarm. It was right in the middle and under an interstate interchange. Crap-freakin' central. The hordes had pushed us back and back and back until we were in the heart of the city's swarm nest. They were literally raining down on us from all the overpasses –exploding like blood slushy water balloons. We were goners, just trying to go out in a blaze of glory with Old Mother Hubbard looking on from her wheelchair. We were dropping like flies, and then all of a sudden, we weren't. They were like a freight train and we were the hobos. Freakin' majestic."

Padre was nodding and watching Gill and Holly ply their trade as he listened to Lee. "Then why cower in fear as the swarm passed the house by? Why come this way at all?"

"Old Mother Hubbard, that's why. Hello!" Lee answered with disgust. "Plus, moods don't last and neither do miracles. We couldn't stay in the city long term."

As they watched, Gill was storming across the field as if she were on horseback and the battle standards of the War Maiden of France were trailing after her. Padre looked at her dumbly for a second, wondering where she had been storing her weapon of choice all this time. It was a bo staff. He had noticed her long legs, as much as a priest could notice such things without causing trouble for himself. But there was no way she could have concealed a whole staff down her jeans, he thought, no matter how long. And then, in a flash, he understood. "Clever girl," he said aloud, though Lee ignored it. Gill carried a collapsible bow staff, like a blind man's folding cane, but stout.

"Watch this," Lee said, removing one hand from his folded arms to point at Holly. The younger girl, Padre saw, was crouched down and fiddling with her Converse All-Stars. "Don't know how she keeps them so white," Lee snorted.

The edge of the oncoming swarm had started tumbling dumbly into the roadside ditch. Louisiana's river roads were lined by minor ravines instead of shoulders. They looked like the helmetless ghosts of World War I-era doughboys staggering through the trenches. Holly had clearly seen this spectacle coming, or else had plenty of experience with the phenomenon. As Padre watched, the high-schooler stood back up after adjusting her shoes. A moment later, the priest thought she had gone mad or else was re-enacting the chimney sweep rooftop scene from *Mary Poppins*.

"Our little Rockette," Lee mused with a fatherly bearing. It slowly dawned on Padre that the girl hadn't been just tightening her shoelaces before battle. She had been *fixing bayonets*. She had somehow managed to secure her knives to the front or underside of her shoes, Padre couldn't tell which. A red-black slurry quickly covered her from the knees down.

She was kicking and sidestepping her way along the side of the ditch. Each time she kicked, or almost every time, one of the zed-heads exploded. *Was she*, Padre wondered to himself, *humming a tune as she went?* Padre crossed himself.

*****

Justin was driving his modified Escalade, thinking about his old blue truck. They had left his truck on the Audubon bridge, using it and other vehicles to create a wall across the bridge. That had been weeks ago, Justin was thinking. It wouldn't stop living people that could climb, but it should be enough to slow the zombies, if not stop them altogether. A random stray, they could take care of that. *When was the last time we checked on the bridge*, he was thinking.

"Heads up, bro." Chet said to Justin, tapping the driver's shoulder before turning in the passenger's seat to check either side of the roadway. Justin shook his thoughts out of his mind to see the dark shape of the rising walls of stacked cars that marked Fort Livonia.

It was just them for this part of the plan. Isherwood's Jeep had peeled away from their little caravan when they passed the factory a couple miles back on the highway. Isherwood had Jarrah and Hoskins along with him. Justin was supposed to give them a couple hours before rolling in with a couple thousand zombies following him. Isherwood and the others thought that, given a couple hours, they could get moving whatever might still be functioning at the factory.

The highway leading to Livonia from the northeast, Highway 984, was nearly completely free of wrecks. The Livonia crew had cleared all the adjacent roadways to build the walls of their fort. It made for easy movement between St. Maryville and Livonia. As they got closer to the stacked car walls, however, they could see that the road was not clear of other things. They could see gray shadows moving along the base of the walls.

Justin checked his watch. "What'd'ya think, Chet? Go time?"

"Is this thing right?" Chet tapped the clock on the dashboard.

"Uh," Justin hesitated. "Just look at mine." Chet looked at Justin's outstretched wrist then to the moving shadows ahead. The road ahead was already beginning to fill with patches of zombies. Chet also looked back the way they had come. There were far fewer of the creatures staggering behind them.

"We're supposed to get there for noon, right?" Chet asked, running some numbers in his head.

"High Noon," Justin nodded. He was watching the nearest zombie, as it stumbled against the wide reinforced grill of his Escalade. "At O. K. Corral, no less."

"Better be better than OK," Chet grumbled. "Yeah, I saw we get this show on the road."

"Okay," Justin answered. "Here's the play …"

*****

About ten minutes later, the Escalade had backed nearly all the way into the thickening crowd. At about twenty yards from the wall of stacked cars, the brake lights kicked on and Chet popped out of the turret at the top of the vehicle. He was not a big man. He had probably just started growing his near-middle-aged paunch when everything started falling apart. He had a dark mop of hair and thick, patchy scruff across his face. He really wished he had a loudspeaker. "Hey!" He yelled. "People in there!"

"Very articulate," Justin murmured from the driver's seat.

"Shut up," Chet shot back in a whisper.

"Livonia people! Can you hear me? Tommy, Phil!" Several acres of zombies were lurching now full tilt towards the Escalade. "We've come to lead this crap away, you got that?"

"Yeah, I can hear you, over. *click-shhh.*" Chet heard Justin say from inside.

"Why didn't you tell me you were just gonna get 'em on the radio? You *jerk.*" Chet kicked at the back of the driver's seat. He could hear Justin giggling in the front seat. A smile, partially of embarrassment, cracked on Chet's face. "Whatever. Not cool, man."

"Hiyo, silver," Justin murmured as he shifted the car back into drive. "Away!" Instead of slamming the pedal down and bursting forward, the SUV began crawling forward. Several blood and mud-stained hands squeaked across the glass windows and thunked against the tires secured around the vehicle's sides.

"Grab the z-sticker," Justin called back to him.

"This is gonna be a long drive," Chet mused to himself, still looking back at the growing throng of zombies dragging their rotted, mostly bare feet after the car. He was slowly pulling a long pole out through the turret hole. It was a beefed-up version of a frog gigging pole. He would use it during the drive to the factory to nudge away any zombie track stars and maybe kill a few in the process.

There was an older, white man stumbling around in a night gown. Somehow, Chet noticed, the old zombie was keeping pace with the car. He stabbed the frog-gigging pole into the man's chest through his ragged and torn nightshirt. "There you go, Ebenezer," Chet groaned as he tried pushing the Dickensian-looking zombie away from the truck. When he tugged the pole back towards him, however, he found he was dragging the man back towards the truck. *Crap,* he thought to himself, *the very first one and gotta get it stuck in his sternum.*

Chet struggled with the old zombie, pushing and pulling on him, as if it were a little dance. "Bah humbug," he groaned.

"Try twisting the pole loose," Justin advised as he sat watching the grisly scene reflected in his side mirror. Whatever Chet did next seemed to work, as the man in the night shirt soon tumbled away, crashing, as he did, into a pack of three zombies.

"Nice," Justin chuckled. "Take out the Ghosts of Christmas past through future, while you're at it."

"Merry Christmas, ya filthy animal." Chet shot back, as he stabbed the pole instead into an eye socket.

# CHAPTER FOUR:
# THE O.K. CORRAL

Isherwood was standing along a metal railing looking northward through the marine binoculars. He was standing on the metal landing of an outdoor stair well. The stairs and platform were bolted to the side of a raised operations facility for the factory. Apart from the operations room, the factory was for the most part entirely outdoors. It was a stone-crushing factory. Four long mountains of gravel blotted out large sections of the sky behind him.

"How far out now?" Jarrah called up to Isherwood. Only a few zombies had stumbled across their path upon entering the tall chain-linked fence that completely enclosed the factory. No doubt this was because the gate was still locked tight. The lock had been a challenge for Isherwood's bolt cutters. Both Hoskins and Isherwood had to pull on the tool's long arms.

Isherwood was now standing at the tallest point in the factory, aside from the tops of the conveyor belts that poured crushed stone onto the peaks of the gravel mounds. He was able to see both clouds of dust approaching the factory. There was one from the north and one from the south. The cloud coming up the highway from the south was closer. This would be Justin and Chet leading a swarm away from their Livonia outpost. Padre, Lee, and the ladies were leading another throng of zombies past Smithfield. Padre had the longer road.

"I'd say Justin and Chet are about a mile and a half off. Maybe fifteen or twenty minutes. Padre's group really only just came into view. They're another hour or so away."

"That should work out." Jarrah said, nodding his head. "If the priest gets here too fast, he'll be pinned between the two swarms. Pinned like a bug. That's no good. Chomp, chomp."

"I get the picture." Isherwood answered, masking his anxiety with frustration at the man's frequent questions. "How's Hoskins coming with getting the power on? You helping him?" But Jarrah didn't answer, having walked outside of earshot. Isherwood guessed he just didn't want to answer.

Isherwood was also in radio contact with both crews. Padre's signal was growing stronger, but there was still a lot of static.

Isherwood took another look at the approaching dust clouds of the two swarms and then lowered the heavy marine binoculars. He turned and tugged on the metal door to the operations control room. Though the factory's fence had been locked tight, the rest of the place was wide open. The workers had obviously left in a rush. Isherwood picked up a fallen clipboard as he returned to the broad panel of displays, dials, and buttons. He look ominously into a mug of coffee that had been left behind in the rush to leave. There was still some coffee left inside, but the remaining liquid had grown a thick, colorful skin of something.

Most of the capability of the operations center was lost without the electrical grid. Nevertheless, they expected some of the place to come back to life once Hoskins got the generators back up and running. He had found plenty of diesel stored in above-ground tanks beside the large shed that housed the generator area. He would likely need to hand crank the gas if refueling was necessary. Nearly all the fuel gauges in the bank of diesel generators displayed at least half a tank.

Isherwood felt a sudden tingling in his feet. The gray, linoleum-covered floor was vibrating. Seconds later, he could hear as well as feel the generators roaring back to life. A row of fluorescent lights sputtered on overhead. Streaks of display lights started buzzing back to life across the operations panel. The door clanged open, and Jarrah glided through the doorway as if on cue. With a distracted hand, he swiveled around and rolled a beat-up officer chair over to the panel. He sat down on torn seat of the swivel chair. Bits of yellow foam upholstery were leaking from the place where the cheap upholstery had been poorly glued to the black plastic underbelly of the chair.

"How far out now?" Jarrah asked again, while pouring over the console. Hoskins voice was crackling now and then through the walkie-talkie at his side. "That's right, 'Skins. Belts, gates, doors, grinders. All up and running, or will be after initialization."

Isherwood was watching Jarrah with his mouth slightly agape. "You, uh – you worked in a gravel factory before or somethin'?"

"Nah," he turned around smiling. "But I've been bounding around for quite a bit. It's not – *wasn't* easy finding consistent work when you look like a terrorist." His smile slackened, and he repeated. "How far?" It was his turn to be frustrated.

Isherwood shook his head to regain his concentration. He grabbed the marine binoculars and again stepped onto the metal landing, wedging the door open behind him. As he scanned the horizon with the massive binoculars – normal binoculars would probably do just as well now – he was reminded of Luke Skywalker scanning the Dune Sea looking for the lost droid. One of the ladies back home – he thought it was probably Aunt Lizzy – had instituted movie night. They had borrowed a projector from the youth room. There was a pull down screen in the Parish Hall. It was every Thursday night, and it had become quite a big deal, especially among the kids. There had been a rainy day just last week, and they had made it into a movie marathon day. Star Wars. They had shown all six episodes from start to finish, right down to the dancing bear party. At the end of it, he had been bitterly reminded of the consequences of the end of the world or at least most of it. The first film of the new trilogy had been ready to hit theatres and never did. They would never know what happened in Episode 7: The Force Awakens. Of all the possible tragedies to consider, this little one, this almost miniscule tragedy, had really shaken him.

"Well?" Jarrah asked again. "You're holding me in terrible suspense."

"Quarter of a mile," Isherwood said, swallowing down the memory. "Justin and Chet are nearly here."

\*\*\*\*\*

"Here comes the Calvery, ur, I mean, cavalry," Isherwood announced. He wondered to himself whether his mistake might prove to be prescient.

He no longer needed the large sea binoculars. Both groups were rapidly approaching. Justin's modified Escalade had just come into sight along the roadway. The vehicle was slowly appearing from behind the narrow stand of trees that lined the shoulder of the road. The swarm oozed from the roadway, filling the shoulder and abruptly ending at the factory's fence. Even now, they could hear the grisly orchestra of hundreds of rotting hands clanging against the chain-link fence.

Chet was still perched inside the turret hollering obscenities at the dead masses as the Escalade rolled slowly towards the open factory gate. There was still another fifty yards or so to go before the vehicle rolled onto the crushed gravel road that led into the factory. The plan was for Isherwood to guide them in from there, if necessary.

"Okay, boss." Jarrah said, giving a distracted salute. "I think this old girl is ready."

"Good, 'cause we've got incoming." As Isherwood watched, Justin sped up a little bit to put some distance between himself and the horde before making the turn into the factory. "Doing good, Justin," Isherwood said into the walkie-talkie. "We've got, just like we discussed, a parking spot on the right side of the chute that should also help block them in, over."

"I'm headed over to the grinder deck," Isherwood announced to both Jarrah and the walkie-talkie. "Y'all should see me as you drive down through the gravel canyon. There's a ladder not far from the parking spot. Take as much ammo as you can from your truck, just in case, over."

Jarrah could hear Isherwood's footsteps as he clanged down the metal staircase. These abruptly ended as he ran off past and around the long gravel mountains to the artificial box canyon they had chosen to lead the zombies into. But soon, another pair of boots started clanging up the staircase. These were going much slowly and were far less *lively*.

Jarrah tried not turning around to face whatever was climbing up those steps. He knew it was just Hoskins. *Man, the old guy sounds like one of them,* he couldn't help but think. This was a critical moment, though. He couldn't just step away from the control panel. Just in case his throat was about to be torn open by zombie, he pressed the round, black plastic button that started turning the great wheels of Grinder #3. The conveyor belt, which led to its yawning black mouth, could only be operated from the grinder platform itself, as a safety precaution. There was a manual override switch, but it appeared to require a key they hadn't been able to locate just yet.

*****

Isherwood stood catching his breath atop the grinder platform. He was in much better shape now than before the apocalypse, but his heart was racing nevertheless. His belly, too, filled with the excitement and panic of several thousand zombies bearing down on them. He had every reason to trust in Padre's plan, but he still felt the dark exhilaration pressing down on his chest.

The platform was vibrating disconcertedly as massive spiked steel cylinders spun beneath him. He put his hand around the metal control box that had been labeled for the conveyor. He pushed another black plastic button and the heavy-weight conveyor belt lurched into motion. Isherwood felt uneasy as he looked down into the black mouth of the machine below. He imagined the geyser of blood that would soon be erupting from its depths as it chewed up an entire army of the dead. He wished to himself that had brought a poncho. *I'm about to see just how curdled their blood really is,* he thought to himself as his stomach lurched.

Beyond the long gravel mountain to his left, the groans of a thousand decaying throats were echoing across the manmade hills. Isherwood could almost imagine a football stadium lay beyond the mountain, filled to capacity with unhappy fans. He was terrified and excited all at once. He stood at the head of an artificial canyon made by two long piles of processed gravel. Each pile was at least two hundred and fifty yards long. There were several of these gravel mountains stacked parallel, one after another like rising and falling waves with maybe fifty yards between crests.

At the end of each canyon were more grinders. If the first zombie swarm didn't fit in the first canyon, they planned on leapfrogging to the next one. Isherwood couldn't imagine that even both swarms together would fill the first canyon. He was more worried about the grinders. He wasn't sure if they could sustain the constant barrage. Hoskins had assured him that these machines could take it, but Isherwood had his suspicions. "Rocks aren't wet," he had told Hoskins. "There's about to be an ocean of liquefied humans running out from this thing and pooling."

Isherwood braced himself along the platform railing as Justin's Escalade rounded the first gravel mountain. Justin had made a wide turn into the canyon so that he was facing straight in. The Escalade paused at the mouth of the canyon. Justin laid on the horn, while Chet kept on hollering from the turret. The first couple of zombies staggered around the curve of the mountain. They fell as the gravel shifted underfoot and were soon trampled underfoot. The leading edge of the horde was clinging tightly to the curve of the mountain. The zombies were grinding up themselves. Even from hundreds of yards away, Isherwood could see how the mountain was being splashed by the dark paint of their blood.

Justin accelerated suddenly as the first twenty or so hands began groping at his back bumper. He was in the home stretch after leading the horde slowly forward for the last five miles. Isherwood suddenly began to worry about Justin's tires over the final stretch. The narrow road between the mountains was typically traveled by heavy duty equipment. It was littered with sharp rocks that could easily pop one of the Escalade's tires. *He just had to get a pretty boy Caddy*, Isherwood thought bitterly.

Amazingly, Justin and Chet pulled into the small space beside the conveyor without a hitch. From above, it looked like the vehicle had plugged the hole out of the canyon perfectly. The conveyor belt was now the only way forward. Isherwood hollered down to the guys in greeting and took over the job of baiting the swarm forward, screaming at them. Justin and Chet meanwhile were grabbing as much ammo as they could from the vehicle.

The way the zombies trampled over one another at the opening of the canyon began to worry him. *What's gonna happen when they get to the choke point?* He was thinking. The conveyor belt was lined with sturdy-looking steel walls, but they ended at the belt. If the walls continued forward, curving gently away from the belt, Isherwood thought, it would have been a proper chute for animals. *If I survive this, I'll know how to make a proper human grinder.*

"You idiot," Justin said, greeting his old friend. His feet banged across the vibrating metal platform. Isherwood could hear the bullets rattling ferociously in Justin's ammo box as soon as he dropped it onto the steel floor.

"Had a nice, leisurely cruise through the country, eh?" Isherwood smiled. He kept hollering and waving his hands to keep the zombies interested, as the other two laid down their firearms along the platform.

"Y'all got this thing running, huh?" Chet asked, joining the other two on the platform. "Wow."

"It was all Hoskins and Jarrah, believe me." Isherwood said as they all started hollering again at the oncoming horde.

"I hate all those white eyes staring at me," Chet said, but the other couldn't hear him over all the racket.

"Hey," Justin called out over the din. "So they just walk onto the ramp, get sucked in, and turn into blood sausage?"

"What?" Isherwood called out, but soon pieced the words together. "Oh, yeah. That's the plan."

"What if they're not all gone when Gill and the others drive in?" Chet asked. "Won't they be stuck in the middle?"

"Keep it up, guys," Isherwood started hollering even louder. "Come on, this *way*," he said, firing a couple rounds into the crowd from his 9mm.

"Who's Gill?" Isherwood asked. "Oh, right. The *redhead*. Hopefully the zeds will all be 'blood sausage' by then, but we've got Hoskins on a second grinder next door and Jarrah's working on a rock slide, too, to trap them in here with us."

"Here we go," Justin said, giddily. He seemed to be the only one unfazed by the idea of being trapped in this space with thousands of undead. "Looks like it'll be door number one for our lucky winner!"

The first zombie fell forward onto the conveyor belt after the sudden change in momentum. The belt stood at a pretty gentle slope, but was nevertheless notched every couple feet to help keep the rocks from backsliding. The notches, they saw, may or may not be helpful for the conveyor's new purpose.

The zombie was back on his feet with surprising speed. It had been an older man, mostly bald and with a white goatee. Miraculously, despite all the miles he had likely staggered, he was still wearing his glasses. The glasses were twin circles of black wire. They fit tightly against the zombie's eye sockets.

"Dude, that one looks just like Elmore Leonard." Isherwood called out, joining Justin at the rail.

"Elmore who?" Justin asked, unable to look away as the zombie was drawn closer and closer to the mouth of the grinder.

"Maybe you should take a step back for the first one," Chet warned. "Don't know what might pop out of these skin bags when smooshed. Might get infected if it hits your eyeball, you know. Like in, uh, *28 Days Later*. Remember the Scottish dude from Braveheart? One drop in the eye and he started twitching."

The other two weren't listening to Chet's ramblings. Their eyes were glued to the Elmore zombie. He was now only a couple feet from the top of the conveyor belt and the sudden fall into the emptiness and then the grinders' teeth.

"Ohhh, man. Here he goes," Justin nearly shrieked in delight.

The zombie seemed to hover at the end of the conveyor belt for an impossibly long time, and then he teetered at the edge. There was no fear registering on his face. He was reaching for the men on the platform the entire time. His distended belly hit the nearer grinder wheel with a splat as his feet fell almost perfectly between the two grinding cylinders. One of the grinder's teeth protruded through his rib cage. Its body pulsed slowly as it was chewed from the bottom up. With each of the pulses, the pressure must have been building in the things body cavity. When the thing's torso was half-devoured, it suddenly exploded. A bulb of shifting tissue emerged from the thing's neck like a massive goiter. It popped and a vertical jet of the zombie's innards shot straight upward.

Isherwood and Justin reeled backward just in time, as a tower of chunky black blood and rot ascended above the platform with a line of intestines serving as the kite's tail. It seemed to hover in the air a second, just as the zombie had a few seconds ago, before falling into the grinder's maw. As it all slowly turned to its descent, Isherwood caught a glimpse of the Elmore Leonard-style glasses glinting in the midday son.

"Did you *see* that?" Justin whirled around in mirth. "Thing popped like a zit! You were right, Chet, old buddy. We were almost splattered with that zit-thing's puss. *Dude.*"

Isherwood watched now a step back from the railing as groups of two and three zombies at a time were loading themselves onto the conveyor belt. The horde of zombies was still rounding the edge of the gravel mountain, but appeared to be slackening in size.

"This plan might just work," Chet said, still wide-eyed.

"Yeah, so long as the back of the horde doesn't lose interest and ..."

"The grinder doesn't clog up," Justin said. "We're gonna need some poles or something in case they start coming too fast or we need to prod something out of the grinder."

"I've got *that*," Isherwood said, pointing to the conveyor belt controls. "We can always turn off the belt if they start mounding up on top of the grinders."

"You'd think we'd be fine," Chet said tentatively leaning over the railing to see how the grinder was handling the increasing rate of falling zombies. "This thing grinds up *boulders*."

"Yeah," Isherwood said, looking down into the machine's mouth. There was a rising mist of body fluids hovering over the grinder. "Thing's doing great, looks like when I put leaves into my wood chipper." As Isherwood watched, the grinder was devouring three or four zombies at a time. Every once in a while, a skull would pop up, rattle around the works like a roulette ball, and then fall into place and get pulverized like it was nothing more than papier-mâché.

Isherwood was dimly aware of Justin climbing off the platform in his search for prodding poles. He took the moment of relative peace to contact the others on the radio. "Swarm one is all in the canyon. Repeat, Swarm One is all in. Padre, you hearing this? Over."

He waited a couple seconds staring at the radio, as if he could make Padre answer by force of will. The radio remained silent. "Hoskins? Jarrah? Are you hearing a response from Padre? Over."

The radio crackled to life. "Nope, nothing." It was Hoskins. "But Grinder Two is ready and rumbling. Over. *click-shhh.*"

Isherwood looked up to the long gravel mountain, wondering if it was blocking his signal. As his eyes trailed back down to the ground, he noticed that not all the zombies were focused on their platform and the conveyor below. A few had become distracted around the Escalade. The parked vehicle wasn't a perfect wall, but it was intended to slow down any zombies that might come from that direction.

"Here," a voice called out. "Grab these." It was Justin, climbing the ladder back up to the platform. All Isherwood could see was the tip of a pole hopping around near the top of the ladder.

Isherwood ran over to the top of the ladder to grab the poles from Justin. "Crap, man. You see what you're doing? Ain't gonna work if I gotta babysit you boys."

"What?" Justin said. He looked down suddenly as hands grabbed around his boot. Teeth clenched around his Achilles' heel. If it weren't for the thick shoe leather, he would have been a goner. He cursed and knocked the thing off with the heel of his other boot. He dropped down to the ground to face the three zombies that had already wriggled through the space between the gravel mounds and his Escalade.

"Chet," Isherwood called out. "Fire a few rounds to keep their eyes on the prize as we clean-up. Okay?"

Chet nodded. The panic was evident on his ghost-white face.

"Push them back to plug up the …" Isherwood started as he jumped down from the ladder, but realized his friend was already a step ahead of him. Justin was just removing his hunting knife from the temple of a stringy haired zombie, after having wedged her body in the narrow space between the vehicle and the base of the platform.

Isherwood's katana sang as it sliced through the air and through the neck of a one-eyed zombie. This one fell where it stood. He pushed the tip of his sword into the exposed rib cage of the second zombie, pushing it around the far side of the Escalade. Isherwood was acutely aware, as he did this, that the underside of the SUV was still unplugged. He just knew a set of jaws was about to close around the meat of his calf.

He grabbed hold of the zombie's reaching hand and steered it backward with his sword. He wedged it backward with a killing blow from the sword. He discovered with a sudden lurch of his stomach that the backward force had sheared off the skin of one of the zombie's fingers that he had been holding onto. In the palm of his hand, he saw the limp tube that had been the skin of the creature's ring finger. The zombie's gold wedding band was also there. He cast them both away with a disgusted twitch.

There was a sudden rush of zombies to either side of the vehicle. "Don't forget to plug up the underside, Justin," he called over the vehicle. He plunged the katana into the heads that were trying to squeeze through the narrowing space. He dropped to his knees to do likewise to creatures that might be crawling under the vehicle.

He was suddenly face to face with a zombie just emerging from under the Escalade. Its teeth snapped at him. Its cold, fetid breath covered his face. He had no room to maneuver his sword in the tight space. He tried crawling backward, but the foot of his boot wedged between two shifting boulders. He was about to add his own body to fill the breach in their wall.

Suddenly, the zombie's nose lengthened as though he had just told a lie. The skin of the nose stretched and then tore clean off, as the sharpened tip of a frog-gigging pole cleaved through the thing's skull.

"I gotcha, bro." Justin said. "Get out of there. I got this."

Isherwood took a moment to rub his forehead where the tip of the pole had almost notched him. He easily dislodged his boot now that his panic had passed. He regained his footing and sheathed his sword. He picked up the remaining poles and loaded them onto the platform, while Justin finished plugging the holes around his vehicle.

He was back on the platform in time to see the swarm's focus shift back to Chet and the platform. Simultaneously, his radio chirped to life. He had dropped it on the floor of the platform in his rush to alert Justin. It wasn't Padre's voice as he hoped. It took him a second to place the woman's voice.

In that moment's hesitation, Chet grabbed the radio from him. "Gill? Is that you? Where are you?"

"Yeah, it's me," the radio squawked. "You're supposed to say 'over,' boy-o. Over. *click-shh.*"

"Right, sure, 'over' – well, now 'over' just yet ..." Chet said.

Isherwood forcefully took the radio back from the blushing young man and scowled at him. "This is Isherwood. Where are you? Over."

"Knocking on the front door. Turning in. You better be ready for us. Over. *click-shh.*"

"Yeah, a little early, but I think we're ready. There's still several hundred of these things looking at us and the entrance to the canyon is still wide open. Drive right past the first canyon and don't dawdle. We'll probably divide your swarm between the first two canyons but that will be fine. Any questions? Over."

"Hoskins here." The radio crackled before Gill could answer. "I'll be waiting for you at the second grinder. Over. *click-shh.*"

"It's a date," Gill answered. "That sound in the background. That was the zombie food processor, wasn't it? Gross. Don't answer. We'll see you in a moment. Over."

# CHAPTER FIVE:

# SLIPPERY SLOPE

Justin stood atop the ladder, trying to scrape his boots along the underside of the platform. "Big ol' puddle starting to form down by the outlet. Goop spilling out like something out of *The Shining*, man."

"Just needs to hold out a little longer." Isherwood said. He didn't know if he was trying to reassure Justin, himself, or the machine below them.

"She's still purring like a kitten," Chet said as something clanged beneath them. His thoughts had clearly been elsewhere ever since Padre's Humvee had driven past the mouth of their canyon, honking as it went. The conflicting distractions had caused some of the horde in the first canyon to turn around, but it had been simple enough to draw their attention back to the platform and conveyor belt below.

They had watched as a good portion of the second horde had followed Padre into the second canyon. A good portion also veered off into their canyon. As Isherwood watched, a thought suddenly slapped him across his face. *The first horde should've gone to the* second *canyon. Then, the first group wouldn't've distracted the second group.*

"Idiot," he said pressing the heel of his hand into his forehead.

"What?" Justin asked, and Isherwood explained his error. "Yup," Justin winced. "That would've been the thing to do."

"But that just means less for other group, right?" Chet asked.

"Right," Justin frowned. "We're up to our eyeballs in ... well, eyeballs. But your girlfriend, she's on Easy Street."

"She's not my ..."

"Whatever," Justin said.

Their clothes were slowly becoming saturated by the low-hanging mist welling up from the grinder. Justin picked up a couple poles, his trusty frog gigging pole and another he had found lying around behind the platform. He handed one to Isherwood, and said "Come on, let's check this out."

The two men leaned over the railing to inspect the grinders. As they did, they were dimly aware of footsteps clanging down the ladder. "Gonna check on the others," Chet yelled to them. Isherwood grunted an acknowledgment, but he had become quickly absorbed in the inspection. There were piles of large, undigested bone fragments lining the inner walls of the grinder. These would need to be pushed into the mouth of the grinder or it would clog. Somehow, they also saw, an entire living torso had managed to wedge itself in the corner of the grinder. The teeth of the grinder had eaten a huge swath of the creature's chest away. Only the back of its ribs were left between its left shoulder and its belly button. It was stuck in a rapid never-ending loop of reaching forward towards the men on the platform and getting thrown back by grinder.

\*\*\*\*\*

Chet made sure that none of the zombies noticed him leaving the platform. He tapped himself making a quick inventory of his weapons. He did this several times. It was a nervous twitch that had followed him into the apocalypse. When he was nervous before, he would absent-mindedly check his pockets for his wallet, phone, car keys, and pen. He didn't have much use for any of these things now. His necessities had completely changed. He had traded his wallet for a 9mm sidearm and his keys for a large hunting knife. He tapped these distractedly as well as his extra ammo, as he jogged around the gravel mountain that stood between the first and the second canyon. It was fifty or so yards around the base of the mountain. The mountains were stacked very steeply, rising almost as high as they were wide.

He was jogging at an easy pace, trying to appear almost casual. That changed suddenly when he heard her scream.

\*\*\*\*\*

No one would have suspected beforehand that it would have been the Humvee, they had borrowed from the National Guard armory, that would have had the most fragile tires. With a sudden jerk, the Humvee's left front tire had blown out. They were only about halfway down the canyon when it happened. Padre was able to coax the vehicle the rest of the way down the canyon, but at a much slower pace. By the time he had slid the Humvee into its appointed parking spot to the left of the grinder, the swarm was nipping at the rear bumper.

"That's far enough!" Gill yelled out as she and Holly spilled out the backseat of the vehicle. "Seal the gaps," she barked at Padre and Lee. The two men obliged the ladies without protest in the sudden panic. Hoskins, for his part, had stayed on the platform and was yelling obscenities into the thick crowd of zombies, encouraging the swarm to stagger onto the conveyor belt.

Lee Majors caught glimpses now and then of the girls plying their trade against the oncoming swarm. It reminded him of when he had first met them. They had been blazing a trail through the swarm of all swarms at the intersection of major interstates in the heart of Baton Rouge. But he was still scared for them. "Come on," he called to them. "We'll just seal the gaps with *them*." It was like a bad dream. No matter how loud he screamed they couldn't hear or wouldn't listen. Padre was also calling to them, too. There were just too many. The dead were pressing in from every side.

Suddenly, the amphitheater of echoing, moaning zombies fell silent. They all quieted, live or dead. Somebody was screaming along the gravel wall on the far side of the grinder. Gill was just yanking her knife out of the temple of a zombie. She looked up suddenly to see Chet's face from across the canyon. He had locked eyes on her for just a moment before turning back around. He was scrambling up the loose gravel sides of the mountain on the opposite side of the canyon. He was screaming as he went, likely due to the pain of scraping his whole body against the sharp rocks. "Go," he yelled to Gill and Holly. "Get behind cover."

Chet wasn't able to grab a firm perch along the steep sides. Besides that, the gravel was eroding quickly beneath him. He could feel the skin tearing away in sheets from his bare hands as he scrambled madly upward. He might lurch upward five or so inches, but then fall backward another six. It was only with great pain that he gained even an inch. Even then, he was moving farther and farther *into* the canyon, away from safety. He was basically climbing on a vertical treadmill. He wouldn't be able to keep it up for much longer. He could feel their hands brushing against the soles of his boots. Another inch, and they'd be pulling at his boots. It would be nothing then for them to yank him down, down into a hundred snapping jaws.

"Chet!" Gill called out. She was already safely on the platform. "Climb, you imbecile. Climb!" She was crying. Tears were making clean lines down her blood and dust-splattered face. They were all yelling now. "Just freakin' hold on, stupid." The redhead grabbed one of the Henry rifles off Padre's back and started firing into the crowd just beneath Chet. She thanked God it wasn't a shotgun as the first dead head exploded.

"No pistols. Not at this range," Padre said putting his hand across Lee's barrel.

"Outta my way," Lee said, pivoting away from the priest with a deranged look on his face. He had put three rounds into two skulls at twenty yards before Padre could say another word. Padre just shrugged and unslung his other rifle.

Somehow, miraculously, Chet was able to push off from the shoulders of one of the headless zombies now resting against the gravel slope. He launched himself five or six inches up the slope. It was just enough to take the edge off his panic. All the gunfire, too, was sending the swarm into a frenzy. The back of the horde was pushing forward so violently that the zombies still reaching for Chet were being pushed past him.

The conveyor belt was packed tight with the onrushing zombies. Half a dozen at a time were spilling into the grinder, their eyes never leaving the redhead with brass-plated rifle.

There was a steady fountain of gore spraying up well above the platform. "Stand back," Hoskins urged them. "Thing's like the bloody Bellagio."

The men still keeping watch at the first grinder would later say that even some of their swarm tried clawing through the gravel mountain to get to the second grinder.

Meanwhile, Chet was delicately inching his way back to safety. Another couple feet and he would be able to slide down the gravel slope behind the corrugated steel wall that separated the swarm from the grinder and the rest of the factory.

As he finally slid to safety, he stood back up to see a flaming head of hair and two violently green eyes. His face was suddenly knocked to the side from a hand he never saw coming.

"You're the stupidest, saddest sack of sh—" Gill was saying before her mouth was slammed with the kiss she never saw coming. Her body tensed up like an iron rail, and then slowly, inexorably melted into the contours of his body. Chet didn't care at that moment or even notice until much later that the palms of his hands were almost entirely worn off. He was leaving bloody handprints all up and down the back of her t-shirt, completely oblivious to the pain.

"I've been meaning to ask," Padre said several minutes later back on the platform. His plan was well in hand. Both grinders appeared to be exerting only minimal effort to chew through the three or four thousand zombies that had been lead to the factory. Jarrah had finally succeeded in creating enough of a landslide to cap the end of the first canyon. "Where'd you learn to shoot a pistol like that?"

Lee's smile seemed, as usual, more like a converted sneer. "State champion pistol shooter, 25-meter rapid fire, two years in a row. Would've gone to the Olympics, too, if it weren't for all the drug-testing."

"Performance-enhancing?" Padre asked.

"Not really."

*****

"Are you *kidding* me?" Isherwood yelled. They had all gathered back in the control tower. It had been an hour or so since the second grinder finished devouring the last zombie trapped in either of the two canyons. Impossibly, the first grinder had actually, finally clogged on the last three or so zombies. Justin and Isherwood had been forced to dispatch these by hand.

It was by now three or four in the afternoon. Isherwood had let the door to the control tower clang shut behind him. He was about to run down the stairs as he had so many times before that day, when he stopped suddenly in his tracks.

There was a burned face staring back at him. It was in tatters. Shreds of skin were dangling from the jaw bone and chin. The zombie had already climbed halfway up the stairwell on its hands and what was left of its knees. There were more, too. Isherwood realized with a flash that they had left the gate open all this time. There had been stragglers from both swarms that had been trickling in all this time, unnoticed. They must have finally coalesced around the control tower with all the celebrating feet banging on the metal floor.

Isherwood nearly tripped as he ran back up the stairway. He thought he could feel hands pulling at the back of his neck and tugging at heels of his boots all the way back up. He reached the little landing at the top of the stairs and tried to soften his steps, albeit too late. He pulled the door closed behind him with a harsh scrape of metal on metal. He winced at the sound as he locked the door. He looked around madly for something to further secure the door with. Finding nothing that could help them with the flimsy knob, he dragged a filing cabinet over to the door and laid it down across the door. He would use it, he thought, as sort of a seed crystal for a mounding up the zombies until they fully blocked the door with their bodies.

"Dude," a voice said behind him. Isherwood turned around to see everybody quietly staring back at him. "Something wrong?" Justin continued with a note of sarcasm.

"How many?" Padre asked.

"Plenty," Chet said, leaning over the control panel to get an angle on the ground below.

Lee was actually sneering this time. "How the *hell* did this happen?"

"Oh, come *on*, nancy boys," Gill grunted. The burned zombie slammed its face against the small reinforced glass panel on the door, leaving behind a sheet of its skin. "We just killed thousands of these things and we're gonna be trapped by the last dozen or so. Don't think so." As she said it, she had pulled out her collapsible bo. With an angry twitch of her arm, the staff burst outward.

Jarrah was kneeling where the filing cabinet had been a minute ago. "He about to start praying or something," Hoskins asked Padre. The priest just shrugged. There were now several zombies banging against the cheap metal door.

"Ah, no, no, no," Jarrah said. As some of the others grouped around the man, who still kneeling on the floor, they saw that the filing cabinet had been standing on a trap door in the gray, linoleum floor. Jarrah was holding the square door ajar by a metal loop handle. Hoskins whistled softly as he leaned over behind Jarrah.

"Just how bad is it?" Holly asked.

"Hundreds," Hoskins answered. "Should've never let ourselves all in one place like this."

"At least," Jarrah added.

"The *hell?*" Lee said, knocking the office chair on its side.

"*Shhh!*" Gill rounded on the man, furiously.

"Like it matters," Lee grumbled, crossing his arms in front of him.

"Come on, guys," Isherwood said. "Let's get after this before it gets dark."

"No," Chet said. He was still leaning over the control panel to look out the window. "Wait. *Look.*"

Holly moved to Chet's side. "What is it? A little boy?"

"It's not an 'it' – he's still alive, I think," Chet said. "Just look at him."

"What's he doing?" Hoskins asked. "Hey, quiet, you idiots. I think this guy's trying to help us outta this mess."

Soon, they were all crowded into the window, like some kind of grim family portrait. Over a hundred yards in front of the tower, there was a man standing at the factory gate. They saw that the man, whoever he was, had closed the factory gate and was now making all the racket he could manage. Already, there was a trail of zombies, like picnic ants, leading away from the control tower to the gate.

"He's not gonna get all of 'em over there." Lee said.

"Yeah, but he'll probably get *enough*." Isherwood said. "Get ready. Once we get off the stairs, run for the vehicles. There's a road going around the perimeter of the factory. We'll get their attention and then leave them at the back of the factory."

"What about the little dude?" Justin asked. "We'll pick him up on the way out, right?"

Isherwood was nodding, but before he could say anything, Jarrah interrupted. "Wait, let's not leave all those critters inside the factory. We may need to do this little maneuver again."

"We'll just mow 'em down. No problem once we're in the open," Gill said shrugging.

"Little dude might not leave us much to do," Chet said. "Look at him go." As they watched, they noticed that there was already a dotted line of dispatched zombies leading away from where the man at the fence was standing.

"He's pretty good with that thing, whatever it is." Lee said. In ones and twos, the zombies were staggering into the fence and then collapsing against it.

"I don't get it," Holly said. "What's happening – what's he doing?"

Justin looked at the younger girl in confusion. "He's braining them with that golden stick-thing. You know, through the fence."

"Seriously?" Holly asked. "It doesn't look like he's even moving it."

Jarrah got back down on the floor by the trapdoor. He opened it just a hair and lowered it again softly. He exchanged glances with Isherwood and Padre and nodded.

There was still a half dozen or more zombies clawing at the door. The door had begun collapsing inward. Arms and withered hands were already reaching into the small control room. Padre and Isherwood were moving to either edge of the doorway. Isherwood could have easily sunk his blade into the first few skulls, but he didn't want to clutter the doorway just yet with bodies to trip over.

"Can't we give it a little more time?" Chet asked, now whispering. "He's – little dude's – gonna have this place completely clear in like just a second."

"We can't just leave him hanging like that," Isherwood was shaking his head. "He might be the one that's surrounded a minute from now. We gotta move when we can move. Rule number 42 of the apocalypse."

"Y'all get ready." Padre said grabbing hold of the doorknob. "Next stop, home. Your *new* home."

They were forming into a semi-circle, all eight of them. There was Padre at the door. Chet, Gill, then Holly were next. Lee, Hoskins, and Justin were in the center with a dozen or knives between them, plus a frog-gigging pole. Last were Jarrah and Isherwood facing the crack in the door.

After a five count, Padre turned the lock in the doorknob. He sidestepped out of the way as the door flung open with the sudden rush of four zombies spilling inside. These were quickly trampled. The semicircle of survivors didn't immediately rush into the breach. They were letting the zombies come to them. Otherwise, the doorway would soon fill up with twice-killed bodies.

Nevertheless, a mound of bodies was quickly filling up the small control room. Jarrah took it upon himself to start sliding bodies through the trapdoor. A second after the feet and legs slid through the little door in the floor, there was a sickening crunch. Five or so bodies later, there was no more crunching sound, just the slap of bodies.

After pushing the legs and waist of a zombie through the trapdoor, Jarrah suddenly leapt backwards. The zombie had suddenly thrown its arms out wide across the opening in the floor. Only one of its arms was actively reaching into the control room. The other arm was mangled by several apparent breaks, one of which was evident from its ulna protruding upward from its forearm like a Wolverine Halloween costume. Jarrah, having passed through a moment or two of mindless panic, suddenly recognized the zombie. It was the first zombie, the one who had been pressing his face against the glass. It had been stampeded when the door opened. That's likely when the thing's arm was mangled, Jarrah thought to himself.

Justin turned and gigged the thing before Jarrah had time for much more revelry. "Focus, will ya?" Hoskins kicked at Jarrah as he momentarily sat back against a filing cabinet. "No time for pickin' daisies."

"Or I'll be pushing up daisies, ain't that right, skins?"

The landing of the stairway had been packed tight with zombies. After they had emptied it and the initial rush was over, the pace of zombies staggering into the room subsided. Jarrah now made sure to skull-tap each body as he dragged them through the trapdoor. Hoskins had begun dragging bodies to him, as well, now that the killing crew seemed to have the job well in hand.

*****

"Hey, buddy," Chet said. "You really did us a solid up here."

After another fifteen minutes, the group had divided up. The killing crew, including Gill, Holly, Lee, and Chet, were chewing up the long line of zombies leading all the way to the front gate. Isherwood, Padre, and Justin left together in Isherwood's Jeep to liberate the other vehicles from their parking spots in the canyons.

"Yeah," Gill shouted, as she slammed her bo staff against a long-haired zombie. The creature's face visibly contorted as the bones receded inward and rearranged themselves. It almost seemed to smile, as its cheekbones collapsed inward. "That was a pretty cool thing you did."

"Oh," the man at the gate said. He had been dabbing madly at his poncho. The soiled Wet-Nap in his hand soon joined a pile of similarly soiled wipes beside the man's feet. "That was," he stuttered, clearly taken aback by the compliments. It was also the first time he had spoken to another living person for some time, unless you counted his screaming at the boat that was passing underneath the bridge several days back. "That was nothing. Happy to help. It's not like I was ever really in danger, you know."

"How old are you?" Holly asked.

"Slow down, chica," Chet scolded. "How 'bout we get his name first?"

"Where'd you come from?" Gill asked. Her gratitude had quickly melted into suspicion.

"Seriously," Lee winced. "Lay off the guy." Lee pulled back on the gate and rolled it open a couple feet. "Get it here, friend. I'm Lee Majors."

"Like the Six Million …" The newcomer asked.

"That's me," Lee answered in his sneering smile.

"I'm Wilson."

Holly turned to Wilson as a zombie slumped to one side behind her and then toppled backwards. "So," she said. "Are you coming with us?"

# CHAPTER SIX:

# HOME AGAIN

"**L**et's just get to Smithfield tonight. Hole up there, pick up the Youngs." Isherwood had suggested. "We'll radio home and let them know we won't get back until the morning."

"It's been a good day," Padre said in answer before getting back in his own vehicle. He would have said, 'nobody died today,' but they had stopped saying that sort of thing. Nevertheless, he quickly regretted even remarking on the day.

It turned out there was to be at least one injury that day, despite their run of good luck. As they were loading up the vehicles, one of the guns misfired. Luckily, it had just been a handgun. Chet collapsed in pain, but they were all relieved to see that the bullet had just sailed through the meat of his thigh, completely missing the femoral artery.

Not much later, they had parked the vehicles on the road in front of Smithfield. They still parked in the Old Blue formation, even though Old Blue had been given to Livonia. The Old Blue formation had taken on new meaning. They wouldn't declare any sort of victory out loud, but they nevertheless parked in the victory formation. Isherwood's Jeep and Justin's Escalade were parked on either side of the road with Padre's Humvee standing in the center and a half-car length behind.

Before they had set foot on the front steps, one of the front doors swung open. It has Hillman, but Miss Abby could be seen just inside the door seated in her wheelchair. "Wasn't expecting you lot for another half hour, at least," the old woman said.

"We caught a tail wind," Padre said, nodding to Wilson, who was still wearing his poncho.

"Is that Joey?" Miss Abby asked.

"His name's Wilson, actually." Isherwood corrected politely.

"No, suh." Miss Abbey said, sticking out her lips over toothless gums.

"She's right." Wilson said.

"'Course she is," Lee said. "Woman never misses a trick."

"Joseph Wilson. Wilson's my last name."

"I'll be damned," Justin said.

"No, not you, chère," Miss Abby said quickly and with a smirk. She turned to Padre, "He's a seminarian, or hasn't he told you yet?" A few of them stopped in their tracks, but most were too tired to wonder at the woman's abilities and too eager to get into the house and maybe a bed. Besides that, there was something incredible spilling out of the house.

"What the ... what is that?" Chet said, wincing as he limped beside Hoskins. "It smells like a miracle."

"Mama's been cooking," Hill said. "Tried telling her to stop, but, well, you can imagine."

*****

There had been a feast that night. Miss Abby had sent Hillman down into what amount to a basement in southern Louisiana. Down a small flight of worn, wooden steps, Hillman had found the root cellar. It had been where, Hill quickly discovered, Smithfield's former occupants had stored the bodies of their dead. They had been properly dispatched. Otherwise, it would have likely been the end of the entire Young family. Once his panic had subsided, Hill realized that the floor of the root cellar was stacked high with potatoes, as well bodies. And then he had seen the true treasure of Smithfield. He had nearly smacked his face into it. The ceiling of the cellar was cluttered with hangars, and the hangars were full of salted and cured meats.

The next morning, they piled into the three vehicles. There was plenty of room for everybody, even enough room for Chet to stretch out his leg. Miss Abby's wheelchair, too, fit easily into the Escalade's cargo area. Isherwood had asked that they leave the cache of cured meat in the root cellar, hoping it might later serve as an enticement to return. He knew they would need Smithfield to become an outpost.

*****

"So relieved to see you all back and unharmed," Patrick sighed in relief as the small caravan passed him. He had opened the back gate of the church parking lot and would slide it back into place as soon as they were all through.

Justin and Isherwood's kids were spilling out of the Parish Hall as the SUVs slid into the open parking spots. Their wives, Chelsea and Sara, both gave up holding the kids back and joined them in lunging for the men. Isherwood's kids were soon plastered against each shin. His boy Charlie was grunting at him to be picked up. He would have to wait, though. Sara had wrapped her arms around her husband's neck and wasn't letting go. "You ... *stop* ... leaving ... us," she was saying between kisses.

"How's the place been holding up without us?" Isherwood asked. "Oh wait, I need to introduce y'all. Lee Majors, Hoskins, Jarrah – this is my family."

"Like the six million dollar ...?" Aunt Lizzy had started to ask.

"The very one," Lee answered with stifled frustration.

Isherwood knew that Miss Abby would be eager to meet Monsignor. The old priest was leaning back against the doorway of the Parish Hall, watching and smiling. Padre and Hill, Isherwood noticed, were taking her right over to the priest.

"Who's that?" Sara whispered as Isherwood took turns hugging his kids and family.

"Yes, Isherwood," his Gran said. "She looks a good twenty years older than me, if that's even possible."

"*Mom*, that's rude," Aunt Lizzy chided. "She'll hear you."

"*You're* the only one not whispering," Isherwood said through gritted teeth, scolding his aunt. "Woman, if anything was gonna teach you how to whisper, you'd think it'd be the zombies."

"That's enough, Isherwood," his Gran said, patting and tugging on his sleeve. "Also, it's time you shaved." Isherwood grumbled in response.

Aunt Tad was going around giving all the newcomers a warm bear hug in greeting. Isherwood made a point to watch Gill's reaction to Tad. He had been expecting the girl to anticipate the attack and step out of the way before Tad could find her. He was surprised to see Tad get the jump on the girl and even more surprised to see the redhead blush and melt a little in response to the affection.

"Come on, now, all you adventurers," Tad announced. "I'm sure we can put some plates together for you in the rectory. There's some newcomers for y'all to meet, too."

*****

"What do you mean 'strange,'" Justin asked Patrick, who had been describing the goings-on since they had left just a couple days ago. Isherwood had asked Tad to take Chet off to attend to his leg injury, while the others were treated to a meal.

"Well," Patrick answered. "Not menacing, exactly. Just strange. We saw the car in the distance and eventually it just drove away. Then, Jerry said he had thought he'd seen something like it before, maybe a week ago. Also, Jett and his wife, some of the new people, said they'd been hearing things."

"Huh?" Jerry said squinting at Patrick. "Oh, yeah. Thought I was just imagining things until Patrick said he saw similar."

"Not much we can do about it now," Isherwood said dismissively.

Lee waved his hand and then said with a mouthful of food, "probably just shy."

"So what's next on the docket," asked Glenn, Sara's dad. Sara's parents and brothers and sisters had joined the others in the rectory. It was where they had been staying while being nursed back to health. The brothers and sisters were well in hand already, as their parents had given them the lion's share of the food. Dale and Missy, however, were slower to recover.

"Hey, how's Missy's arm doing?" Isherwood asked. The only injury, apart from Marshall's death, in their rescue of the LaGrange family had been Sara's mom's arm.

"Still gone, I'm guessing," Justin interjected with a smirk and then immediately regretted it. Glenn gave Justin a look before answering. Justin winced and looked away.

"She's getting along just fine," Gran said.

"We're both nearly recovered," Glenn added.

"Good," Isherwood said. "We're gonna need your and the boys' help with our plans for the cattle and livestock."

"There's something I've been wondering," Monsignor said from the head of the table. He was holding his hands in front of him. As he began to speak, he leaned forward heavily onto his elbows. "You know, this town has an airport."

"Sure," Isherwood was nodding. "We had talked about using it for cattle since it's the largest fenced-in area around which also has a fence taller than the zombies."

"Well, that may be, as well, but I was thinking the airport might be more useful as an airport," Monsignor said, grinning down the table at Miss Abby.

But we don't have any pilots," Isherwood said. "… Do we?" He, too, was now looking down to the old woman in the wheelchair.

Everyone was slowly looking to Wilson, who was holding a plate and standing beside the buffet table, as there were no seats left at the table. "Don't look at me," he said, when he realized people were beginning to stare at him. "I'm scared to death of flying. Much rather walking."

"Well, *who* then?" Patrick asked. "Is it you, Ish? You were always picking up new things."

"Not me, though you're right. I wouldn't mind learning," Isherwood answered.

Eventually, everybody turned back to Miss Abby. "Ah, no," she said. "Ain't my place to say."

"Seriously?" Gill said. "Nobody's fessin' up? Whatever."

"There is another matter, even if the pilot among us wishes to stay anonymous, *for now*." Monsignor said the 'for now' with a certain gravity. "Vanessa brought this to my attention. She says the airport's radio equipment would be far superior to anything we've yet collected."

Isherwood sighed heavily and rubbed his scalp in irritation. "Of *course*," he said. "Why didn't I think of that?"

"Don't blame yourself," Sara whispered to him.

"Just makes me wonder," Isherwood said turning to his wife. "What else am I missing?"

"How could anybody answer something like that?" Sara grumbled. "Honey, maybe it's time you left the front line for a bit. Give yourself a chance to mull things over. See what you might be missing." As she spoke, her hand was rubbing her husband's neck and then his head. She had never felt his muscles so tight before. Even in times of stress in the old days, his muscles stayed pretty loose. Isherwood's head started lolling to one side. Sara had always been amazed at how quickly she could put him to sleep with a neck massage. It was like tucking a hen's head under its wing, she thought with a smile.

When Isherwood and Sara turned back to the conversation, Jarrah was volunteering to help with the communications equipment at the airport. Glenn was volunteering himself and his boys to round up all the remaining livestock in the area. Glenn liked Isherwood's idea of repurposing all the neighborhood fences as livestock pens, as well as building long sections of walls. He wasn't so sure, though, about the chicken coop plan to distract the so-called "river dead."

"There's also another matter," Monsignor began again. "The St. Francis Chapel. It needs to be cleansed. It was once and I'm sure will remain the oldest continuously used church building in all the Louisiana Purchase. I would do it, the cleansing that is, but I'm afraid an old man like me isn't much use beyond the walls these days."

"I'll take care of it, Father," Padre said. He was usually not one to speak up in large groups and usually didn't say much at all unless addressed directly. "Good fence around the chapel, too, if I remember."

Most of the rest of the lunch conversation consisted of Glenn asking questions about the farming operations. He was keenly interested in Isherwood's plan to make the town an island between False River and the Mississippi River. Isherwood returned again to the old map of the area, as he had only a week before. He explained how the Morganza and Smithfield outposts were pivotal for sealing off the island. These two sites covered the gaps of land that prevented the lake and the river from making a complete circle. The Livonia Fort was also critical as sort of a forward base of operations. "It's sort of a lightning rod for any hordes that might otherwise overrun us," Isherwood explained. "Livonia gives us a heads-up, as they did just a day ago. It kept the swarm busy while we put our 'clean-up' strategy together. The gravel factory strategy might well be used again. We ought to think seriously about posting people at Smithfield and the factory going forward."

Midway through what amounted to a PowerPoint presentation in the post-apocalypse, he decided his wife was right. It was time he had a furlough from the ongoing battle against the zombies. He had found reinforcements, lots of them. They all seemed more than capable of continuing on without him. He was struck momentarily by the fear of being replaced as the leader of this place. Then he remembered, it was Monsignor, not him, who really led this place. *Besides*, he thought, *that's ridiculous. My ideas aren't the only good ones around here.* He started wondering, had he even really thought about the airport's potential until now.

The newcomers from Baton Rouge, especially Lee, were also wondering how this monastic idea would work. "I've never been much of a church guy," Lee said with a disgusted frown. "But," he paused. "Being around Miss Abbey has me thinking and rethinking."

There was a mixed murmur in response to this. "So what?" Gill asked. "I've gotta start wearing a long dress or something?"

"Church is just so stuffy," Holly whined, as she picked at her nails.

Jarrah was laughing, "A Muslim convert? Is that what I'm becoming? *Insh'Allah*," he said, throwing his hands into the air.

"You're all welcome here, as well as to the Church," Monsignor said after everyone had finished laughing. "After nearly eighty years, I'm not about to start forcing religion on people *now*. Morning prayer and Vespers, as well as Daily Mass, is a good way to structure our days and our community, but I promise nobody will be whipping you with rosary beads if you miss. Just please wait to receive the Eucharist until you've been received into the Church."

"Monsignor is absolutely right," Miss Abby said, nodding deeply. "More is coming, too, and they'll all be fittin' in. Jus' like he says."

"How many more?" Mrs. Lorio, Isherwood's grandmother, blurted out.

"I see," Monsignor said, wrinkling his brow. "How do you know, Abby?"

"They come to me in my dreams, chère," she said. "It's much clearer when I'm sleeping, but certain things still stick out."

"This is like *Field of Dreams* or something," Patrick mumbled. "If you build it," he said trailing off.

"They *come* to you?" Monsignor asked. Then, with a smile, he added, "Maybe we won't be needing the new radio equipment after all."

*****

It was getting late. Miss Abby had apparently fallen asleep, and little bursting sounds kept popping from her lips. She was snoring ever so softly. Aunt Tad and Gran had started picking up everybody's plates, and everyone started drifting away from the table. Just as Glenn was getting up, Miss Abby woke up.

"Glenn," she said. "Wait. Grab your sista, too."

"Wha …?" Glenn said surprised and a little spooked by the old woman's sudden return to consciousness. "Oh, you mean Tad?"

"Yes'm," she nodded.

"Okay, sure. Give me a moment." Seconds later, Glenn returned from the kitchen. Tad peaked in from the kitchen. She took one look at Miss Abby and started taking off her apron. Soon, they were both sitting at the table on either side of the old woman in the wheelchair.

"What did you need from us, dear?" Tad said, squeezing Miss Abby's hand.

"There's something I've been carrying with me since Baton Rouge. Chet, too," she said, nodding toward the one other person sitting at the table.

Glenn and Tad's heads swiveled down the table to Chet. They hadn't even noticed he was there. Chet nodded back. He was having difficulty looking at them in the eye.

"What is it, miss? Please. I'm not enjoying where this is going."

"It's about your sister," Miss Abbey said.

"Tad?" Glenn said looking over to Tad.

"No, chère. Not Tad."

"Please, Miss Abby," Tad said. "We have … *had* … quite a lot of sisters."

# CHAPTER SEVEN:

# GAS STATION

For the first time, Isherwood was standing beside his wife and waving while others were leaving. Padre had waited until after Morning Prayer and breakfast to lead a group out to the airport.

It felt weird not being with them, but it felt good, too. He never liked leaving his family. So much of his family had survived. It was as rare a luxury these days as a fresh Happy Meal, and he had barely taken the time to enjoy it. He was about to do just that. He and Sara were headed to the church's bell tower for a long-awaited coffee date.

Sara was still using the church's steeple as a lookout point, which was well-suited for her skills with a bow. They could see most of the town from this height.

"Man, the roads look great," Isherwood said after taking a long sip of his coffee.

"Yeah," Sara answered. "Uncle Jerry's pretty good with a pile of bodies on that new tractor of his."

"He's burning them?"

"I think so. We see the smoke ever so often," she paused, grabbing her husband's arm. "We always have the most romantic conversations."

Isherwood snorted on his coffee. He was quiet for a time after that, looking down onto the lake spreading out before them like a giant smile or frown, depending on your perspective, and the restaurant where their rehearsal dinner had taken place. "Remember when we'd spend our morning coffee dates checking our Facebooks on our phones?" He asked.

"Things changed fast and hard," Sara agreed. "Not *all* things for the worse, though. The death of social media wasn't so bad, I guess, like quitting heroin. Watching all this unfold on Facebook and Twitter was insane, though, remember?"

"Hashtag real zombies, hashtag apocalypse nigh ... Yeah, I remember. The videos were terrible. Remember that live feed one of my college buddies posted. He dropped the phone or something, and it just kept recording."

"Turned into a real 'live feed,'" Sara said with a shiver.

"People just stopped posting after a while, like a wheel that slowly stops turning after a car wreck. It lasted for a while, though." After a few minutes of quietly sipping his coffee – Sara had already finished hers – he asked, "How are the kids doing with all this?"

Sara breathed in sharply. "Kids are kids, you know. They adapt so quickly. It helps being at the church, though, someplace familiar to them. I actually think Emma is enjoying the change. She gets to see Gran and the family much more often now."

"She still call them the 'cut men,'" Isherwood asked.

"Sometimes," she laughed. "Her vocabulary has really expanded hanging out with Justin and Patrick's kids."

"Oh, *really?*"

"Yeah, the other kids are starting to get restless and with that, mischievous. All the mothers, we're talking about getting school going again."

"More trade skills than before, I hope. Jerry needs to teach the kids – heck, all of us – everything he knows about welding and farming before he croaks."

"Hey," she scolded. "He's still got plenty of good years left."

"Hopefully so," he backtracked. "But still." Isherwood took down the last sips of his coffee in a gulp and tucked the empty coffee mug in a corner of the bell tower. "You, uh, you like having your family back?" He said, repressing a smirk.

Sara pulled him close in response. "I don't think I'll ever finish thanking you, Isherwood Smith."

"They're my family, too," he said, shaking his head. "Can't tell you how glad I am to have your dad here. He might need to teach a few classes, too."

"Apprenticeships, more like," she corrected.

"That's exactly right," he said, inspired by the thought.

Sara shook his arm to bring his thoughts back to her. "Pretty exciting that we haven't had many zees along the fence, isn't it?"

"Zees, huh?" he asked.

"Yeah, zees, zeds, zed-heads, ZZ tops, zips ... we have all sorts of monikers floating around."

"You know what I'm gonna do today?" Isherwood said with sudden excitement.

"Oh! That must be the coffee kicking in."

"It *is*. I feel like the blood vessels just opened in my brain. I'm gonna get maps and start designing this community of ours. Where the first round of walls will go,

S. L. Smith

for one, and what fields there are in the city to farm." He made to turn and climb down from the bell tower.

"Not so fast, Ish," she said, snapping him back to her side. "You're still on the clock with me," she said pointing at the next highest point in the town, the clock tower of the parish courthouse.

"But that clock stopped working *weeks* ago," he protested.

"And who's fault is that?" Sara said accusingly. "Not *mine*."

\*\*\*\*\*

Padre and his small team stopped at the gas station at the end of Hospital Road before driving the rest of the way to the small airfield. It was the same station that Isherwood, Justin, and Patrick had filled up at before Jerry had claimed his tractor at the nearby John Deere dealership. There had still been quite a crowd of zombies back then. That had been after they led thousands of them over the bridge, trapping them across the river.

"While you two get the gas," Gill was saying to Padre and Lee. "Holly and me will load up supplies from the store, capisce?"

Padre looked to Lee to see if he thought he could cover him without their help. Lee nodded back, and called over, "Yeah, you go ahead. Grab me some smokes, okay?"

Gill made an "okay" with her left hand. "Natty Sherms, right?"

"Black and Gold, if they got 'em," Lee said, as he took aim at the first encroaching zombie. An older man in ragged overalls was stumbling through the ditch across the road. It was still thirty or thirty five yards away. He had switched out his handgun for one of the many .22LR rifles since it was so much quieter. With the scope, he could still freehand headshots at over one hundred yards with little difficulty. His pistol shooting skills more or less transferred to the rifle, but he still kept a pair of pistols in underarm holsters.

"You got this, father?" Lee asked. Padre was already cranking on the hand pump.

Padre nodded. "I'm good for ten or fifteen minutes at least."

"Sounds good," Lee said. "I'm just gonna step into the road for some practice with this rifle."

\*\*\*\*\*

"Ring a ding-ding," Gill said, as the door slammed closed behind her and several bells wrapped around the door handle clanged noisily.

"Hey, look at all these knives," Holly said, as she spun a display case around on the front counter.

"You know those are all crap," Gill said, as she slid the collapsible bo staff from her belt.

54

Holly frowned back at the older girl. As she turned, she let her arm drag the plexi-glass display case off the counter. In a moment, the case was slamming against the floor with an echoing thud. The plexi-glass didn't shatter, but the case's cheap hinges did. "But they're so pretty, Gill," Holly said rummaging in the mess she had made on the floor. "Look," she said. "A *Pokeman* knife. This is an absolutely crucial accessory for the apocalypse. Come on," Holly was saying as she turned and clipped the funny little knife atop Gill's jeans. "Chet will think it's so-oo cute, once his boo-boo is all healed up."

"Shut up," Gill blushed.

"You know," said Holly. "For someone with such fair skin, you don't blush much ... until recently."

"Watch *out*," Gill blurted out. Holly's giggling fit abruptly squelched in her throat. She spun around in time to see a hobbled zombie staggering around the corner of the counter. Its backbone had been mangled somehow and it was staggering at a gruesome angle. If it weren't for the ruined knife display, it likely would've collapsed forward onto Holly's lower leg and started gnawing.

Holly dove to one side in time for Gill to bring her bo down in wide crushing arc. The thing's skull sagged softly inward in contrast to the loud *thwack* made by Gill's bo.

Gill was laughing at Holly as she scrambled to regain her footing, "Who's blushing now?"

"Jerk," Holly said with an embarrassed smirk, as she righted the bulky glasses on her face. She stalked over to the bank of freezer doors and pulled on the door. It was still habit for her to yank on the door to overcome the suction, but the door instead lurched open with the yank and groaned on its hinges in protest.

Holly grabbed a warm Coke Zero out of one of the long, angled trays. As she yanked the bottle towards her, a hand banged clumsily through the narrow opening between the trays and knocked the bottle out of her hand as it reached for her. She yelped in fright and then cussed pathetically as she watched her Coke bottle fizz and explode on the store's floor in the half light.

"*Girl*," Gill shouted. "How many dead stock boys you gonna run into like that?"

"It's just ... how many times did people get zombified in a stupid, c-store freezer?"

"Watch out," Gill cautioned.

"Yeah, yeah," Holly said as the thing came slowly spilling through another gap between the trays. Yoo-Hoo and Starbucks bottles can skittering off the shelves, as the zombie wedged itself through. The shelf quickly snapped off as the thing kept jamming its body through the impossibly tight space. The shelves under it quickly gave way, too, as the falling zombie gained weight and momentum. "Come on, little pumpkin head," Holly was saying, as she put the freezer door between herself and the emerging zombie. The zombie lunged out head first, and the girl caught it between the door and its brass-colored frame. After a few slams, the skull collapsed inward and the madly lurching stock boy finally stilled.

Holly stuffed the body back into the freezer with her foot. As she did, she grabbed a replacement bottle out of the freezer.

"Going with the real deal this time?" Gill asked, as she stood watching the whole spectacle with her hands on her hips.

"Yup," Holly said, puffing stray strands of hair from her face. The bottle fizzed violently as the girl torqued the cap open. "That aspartame stuff will kill 'ya, didn't you know? Besides," she said, hoisting her blue jeans back over her hips. "Think I'm losing weight."

It turned out there was only one more zombie in the place. Moments after Holly's scuffle in the freezer section, they noticed a slow banging coming from the bathroom area. The store's former occupants had managed to confine what was now a zombie into the woman's bathroom by wedging a mop handle through the door handle and an adjacent fire extinguisher hanger. The thing was slowly trying to squeeze its softened skull through the narrow gap in the doorway. It was easy enough for Holly to stab a knife through the space.

There were a few duffel bags for sale in the small sporting goods section. They loaded these up with canned goods. Gill also grabbed all the various flavors of Doritos chips.

"Whoa, gotta love Louisiana," Holly shouted as she discovered a stash of ammunition for sale behind the counter. It was mostly shotgun cartridges, but she sacked it all up. As Holly was leaving, she grabbed the Nat Sherman cigarettes for Lee, as well as some American Spirit for herself. When they left, there was still plenty left in the store. As with the rest of the town, there had been very little looting.

Padre was still pumping when they emerged from the store with their third load of goods. He had just finished filling up the main tank of his Humvee, as well the auxiliary tank. They had recently discovered the second filler tube at the rear of the vehicle. They had later found the "FUEL AUX" switch on the instrument panel. Between the two tanks, the vehicle, Padre had guessed, held about fifty gallons.

As the girls approached with plastic bags bursting with supplies, Padre was just calling Lee over to switch off pumping duties with him. They had five extra six-gallon red fuel tanks to fill, as well, and bring back to the church.

There was a nice line of bodies beginning to mound up on the gas station side of the roadway, Padre observed as he pulled out one of his Henry rifles. He walked over to one of those flashing arrow signs with the illuminated message board. He leaned across the top of it, preparing to use it as a rifle rest.

There was now a steady pace of zombies staggering towards the gas station, mostly all of which were coming down Hospital Road. The town, Padre thought, now seemed to be clearing up. There were at least no more large swarms, though they must not let their guard down. He, for one, wouldn't feel truly comfortable until they had built some more walls. *A lot* more walls.

About twenty rifle shots later, Lee called over to Padre that he was ready. As the priest turned back to the gas station, he could just see the fence of the airport crawling along the horizon in the distance beyond the fields behind the station.

He was suddenly struck looking at the fence in the distance. He stopped in his tracks. His arms were frozen above his head in the act of replacing his rifle in its holster.

"Padre?" Lee asked timidly. The doors to the Humvee clanged open as the ladies leaped back out. In a flash of red hair, Gill was across the parking lot and over to the side of the gas station. She, too, was frozen at the sight.

# CHAPTER EIGHT:

# THE SCHOOL

After another moment, they had all shaken themselves back into action. They had all rushed back into the Humvee. Lee splashed diesel everywhere as he quickly coiled up the hoses and tossed the hand pump into the cargo area of the vehicle. Padre helped him load the red fuel tanks into the back, as well, crushing a few bags of Gill's Doritos in the process.

"How they hell did we miss all that?" Gill said, leaning in from the back seat. Padre and Lee, however, weren't talking at the moment. Their voices were still caught in their throats.

The Humvee lurched back onto the roadway and idled there, like a dog that's been shooed off but only so far. Padre and the others stared into the fields behind the gas station.

"It's not that we missed it," Padre said, staring into the distance. "It's that *that* many were out there at all." As he spoke, there were rows and rows of zombies trudging towards them across the open field. They had been so focused on Hospital Road that they hadn't seen the approaching swarm. Lee's first rifle blast must have drawn their attention, with each successive shot drawing more and more. The leading edge had only now arrived at the back of the gas station.

"What?" Holly was asking. "What's that mean?"

Padre was slowly letting off the brake as he spoke. "It's not a random swarm. They're coming from the fence surrounding the airport. *Something* has been drawing them *to* the fence."

"And for a very long time," Lee said, swallowing hard.

*****

After radioing the situation back to St. Mary's, they decided to lead the newly discovered swarm farther up the Morganza Highway. After a half mile or so, they would cut across the narrow strip of land between the highway and the River Road and then double back to the airport. Padre was obviously wary of leading several hundred zombies toward what remained of his congregation in Morganza, but there were still several miles between there and here.

They were to radio back updates to St. Mary's regularly. St. Mary's, for their part, would inform all their other bases and outposts, especially St. Anne's, of the new swarm. If Padre's group missed more than one scheduled update in a row, St. Mary's would immediately send a crew to intercept them. As it was, however, Isherwood told them he would be setting up a defensive line near the gas station. Padre's group was to fall back to Isherwood's position if overwhelmed.

Isherwood, as de facto commander of all the outposts, decided he wanted to keep the swarm away from the center of town. They had been building new defensive perimeters through the town, including barrier walls, but he didn't want the new walls tested just yet. There were still gaps.

"I don't understand," Gill was asking inside the Humvee. "What would've been attracting all those zees to the airport? You thinking there's survivors inside the fence?"

"Could be that there *were* survivors at one time," Lee said. "But not anymore."

"Nah," Gill said. "They get distracted after a couple days, at least."

"Maybe somebody left a TV on or a radio, and it hasn't thunked off yet," Holly said, as she downed the last swig of her Coke and shove it somewhere.

"Back up power, maybe. It's possible," Lee mumbled. "I'm hoping for survivors, though, like the *pilot* kind."

"If it'd've been a pilot, don't you think he would've flown the coop by now?" Gill asked.

"Maybe he flew in and got stuck," Lee shrugged. "Injured or something."

Padre was slowing down. They were about midway between Morganza and the airport. "Will that take us to the levee road? Looks pretty rough," Lee frowned. "What was that? A prison?"

"A school," Padre answered.

"Looks like the sheriff or the guard or somebody tried turning it into a shelter," Gill thought aloud. "Not successfully. Hope we can get through."

The road was littered with abandoned vehicles. The Humvee was clipping off side mirrors as it went and even grinding against some of the sides of the cars and smaller trucks. "My guess," Lee said. "This is where people went that had no other place to go. Little to nothing packed in these vehicles."

59

"I think this was the backup shelter," Padre said. "After the elementary school and the civic center fell apart."

"Look," Holly said. "The doors. They're moving."

At her words, the others' blood ran cold. As they looked to where the girl was pointing, they saw what appeared to be the school's main doors. They were chained shut, but heaving as something enormous pushed against them from the inside.

Gill cursed. "They probably heard us bumping against the cars."

There were symbols spray-painted in orange around a large 'X'. It would be a poignant image for any person from southern Louisiana. The same symbols were used to mark the houses of the dead following Hurricane Katrina. There was a difference, though. These doors were marked, as well, with another message. In black, dripping spray paint was written "KEEP OUT DEAD INSIDE." Bloodshot and yellowed eyes flashed across the reinforced windows of the doors, rising from the darkness within like messages from inside a Magic 8-Ball.

"Let's just ease on by *real* quiet like," Lee whispered. "Try not to knock anymore of the cars in case an alarm—" Even as he said it, the passing Humvee lightly tapped an old Toyota Tercel. It started howling immediately.

The eruption of sound sent the zombies into a frenzy. The metal doors started contorting and bending, as though struck from inside with a battering ram. Little puffs of dust started spilling from the hinges as their anchor bolts writhed inside their sleeves. The chains, still holding strong, began to tear off the door handles from the rest of the door. In his side mirror, Padre watched as the airport zombies arrived. They spilled into the narrow space between the abandoned cars.

"Just get us out of here, father," Holly said with rising panic, "and I'll convert to whatever religion you want."

The doors burst open like the wings of a flushed bird. They would have bounced back closed, but for the onrush of bodies from inside the school. The first several zombies were ground underfoot as they fell forward. The zombies streamed from inside like an uncoiling snake.

Padre eased serenely onto the accelerator. It moments like this, he had the sense that something or somebody else was guiding his actions. The Humvee was accelerating slowly. They could see the road beginning to curve up ahead as it turned into the levee road that would lead them back to the airfield. All eyes were on the road ahead. As their angle slowly shifted, each of them could feel a heaviness dropping into the pits of their stomachs. By someone's, likely a dead someone's, boneheaded design, the road ahead had been repurposed as a parking lot. The cars were wedged in so tight, they wouldn't be able to walk between them.

"Who the *hell* wedges cars in like that?" Lee was shouting, as he started pounding his fists against the dashboard.

"Can you, uh, can this thing drive over one of the tinier cars?" Gill was asking. "Or ram it out of the way?"

"There's no room to maneuver," Padre answered. "We have two choices, maybe three. We stay inside this tank and use up all our ammo, hopefully it's enough. We abandon the vehicle hear and run for St. Anne's—"

The first several rotting hands slapped against the back of the vehicle, interrupting the priest as they all jumped at the sound.

"St. Anne's, my church, it's only a few more miles down that road," Padre said pointing his thumb westward.

The din of the converging hordes was growing louder and louder. Padre was having to yell just to be heard over the angry moans.

"And the third option?" Gill said.

"We get down and hide in the vehicle. A couple of us bug out as a diversion, leading the horde away and past St. Anne's. Whoever's left in the vehicle catches up with those on foot by taking side roads."

Holly had been holding the door handle with one shaking hand while her other hand had been pulling it back. She was having a panic attack. She wanted to get out of the vehicle. She couldn't breathe inside of it. The cavernous vehicle was collapsing in on her. Upon hearing Padre's third option, her resolve and composure vanished. She through her door wide open and dashed out of the vehicle. She jumped atop the Nissan Sentra that stood between the Humvee and the open fields west of the school. She hiked up her sagging jeans over her hips and started waving and cussing at the hordes. She kept cussing at them even as her lungs seemed to lock up. The cars were parked so tightly, bumper to bumper, however, that the line of cars served as a pretty effective barricade.

Meanwhile, inside the vehicle, Gill just stared at the door that Holly had left wide open. Still staring at the door, she started unhooking her seatbelt and began scrambling over the high platform that ran down the middle of the vehicle's interior.

Lee cussed. "Wha—where are you? But you're *girls*," he finally spat out, protesting. "We can't stay while you all …!"

"Shut up," Gill said, turning around after jumping out the backseat door. "This isn't a feminist thing. You better turn off this vehicle and hide your skinny butts. That's my sister out there, or, uh, as good as, and she's not going out there alone *without me*. Padre's the only one that knows the roads, and you," she said, wincing as she looked at Lee. "You're no – this ain't for you, buddy."

"*Here*," Padre yelled as Gill was turning away. He was pushing something towards her. "Take a radio." Gill rolled her eyes as she grabbed the radio and thrust it down into the front of her tucked-in flannel shirt. In a flash she had spun around, slammed the door, and was standing beside Holly. Padre shut off the engine, as Lee started scrambling into the backseat. All the doors were locked tight. They watched as the horde grew thick around the Nissan Sentra that the girls were standing on. They could feel the Humvee lurching sideways inch by inch as the horde pressed in. The same force was lurching the Sentra and the vehicles in front and behind it forward, as well, but several feet at a time. They saw as Holly stumbled off the far side of the Sentra losing her balance, but Gill was quickly there beside her, leaving a red streak of ponytail in her wake.

"It's working," Lee whispered, unsure if Padre could even hear him over the sound of metal scraping against metal and glass breaking. The horde had not only pushed the line of cars out of the way, it had rolled several of them. The Nissan Sentra, Padre saw as he peaked over the window sill, had rolled two or three times. It was now laying upside down in the field several car lengths away.

There were hundreds and hundreds of zombies still streaming past the Humvee. All of them were bent towards the two young ladies, snapping their jaws at the fresh meat. Padre caught just a glimpse of the two girls running across the field. Lee, who was still crouching on the school-side of the vehicle, was struggling to get a look at the girls' progress.

"Can you see 'em?" Lee asked. "Are they okay?"

Padre nodded quietly in response. "They still coming out of the school?" He asked.

"Petering out, but still coming," Lee whispered as he craned his next to look behind the vehicle. "Must be eight or nine hundred of those things all told. Wish we could just put 'em all back in that school."

"It's an idea," Padre said.

After another ten minutes or so, the bulk of the swarm had passed the Humvee. The field was still full of zombies. Padre watched as they tripped over the deep furrows that ran the length of the weed-strewn field. The onrush of zombies had broken through the line of cars that had hemmed in the Humvee in the first place. The military vehicle could now easily pass through the gap made by the rolled Sentra. It could cut across the field or around it and climb onto the levee road.

Padre knew he could use the levee road to get to Morganza before the girls did. He could scoop them up and still have enough time to investigate the airfield. Only, this would leave nearly a thousand zombies roaming around near his church at St. Anne's. That option was unacceptable.

Lee had been staring at the school's entrance for a while now. He was trying to piece together what had happened here and how things went sour. There were tents set up inside the fenced-in sections of the school that might have served as triage for the wounded. The problem could have easily started there. Some of the wounded likely had undisclosed bite wounds.

The shelter looked like it had many resources that would have helped it to succeed. It was a well-organized shelter for a hurricane, maybe, but not zombies, Lee thought. There was an eighteen-wheeler still full of supplies. At this, ideas started popping through his head like a string of fireworks. He couldn't see inside the truck, but it must be nearly full. He knew this because he could see it was still being unloaded when disaster struck, presumably. There was a forklift seemingly frozen in time, still carrying a plastic-wrapped pallet of supplies. A trail of blood was leading away from it. *Idiot,* Lee thought. *That guy would've been sitting pretty in there.* The operator's seat of the forklift was protected by a shield of plexi-glass as well as a high gauge wire cage.

"Hey, speaking of ideas," Lee said, nudging Padre. "I think I've got something."

*****

The radio Gill had tucked inside her shirt suddenly crackled to life. "Gill, come in. This is Padre, over. *click-shh.*"

"I'd almost forgot it was in there," Gill said, cussing and almost stumbling at the surprise. Holly was beside her. They were keeping pace at a light jog maybe twenty yards in front of the swarm. The swarm had thickened up into a solid mass spanning the entire roadway. Holly was beginning to show signs of tiring, but her panic attack had passed, thankfully, and there was no immediate cause for alarm.

"Yeah, what's up, Padre? Over." Gill said. She was suppressing all the sarcastic comments that had originally come to mind.

"How're y'all holding up? Over. *click-shh.*"

"Just fine and dandy," she answered with a twang. "Where's this church of yours? For that matter, where's this town we're supposed to be running into? Over." And then after a pause, she added, "Hey, *wait*. You gave me your radio, how're you talking to me? Uh, over."

"I'm on Lee's walkie. Plus, the Humvee has a CB, so we can talk to home base, too. Anyway, here's the plan, that swarm is too big for St. Anne's. I'm getting the Humvee back on the road, coming your way. We'll try to turn the swarm's attention back to us and get 'em off your tail. Then, we'll lead it back to the school. Lose the swarm by crossing over to the levee road and head back here, okay? Over. *click-shh.*"

Gill and Holly exchanged looks of suspicion. "What's a levee?" Holly asked between breathes.

Gill looked at her wild-eyed. "You grew up in Louisiana and you don't know what a *levee* is?"

"Nah, just moved here from Dallas before all this crap," she said.

Gill rolled her eyes. "Well, *that* is a levee," she said pointing off to their right. "That long hill back there behind those houses. You *do* know the Mississippi River is just on the other side of that, right?"

"The *what*? Over *there*?" Holly immediately regretted admitting to her ignorance. It seemed to her that Gill's hair and face both pulsed red at her.

"Yeah," Gill said into the radio, ignoring the conversation left hanging with Holly. "We can manage that. Over and out."

Just as Gill released the button on the radio, she noticed that Holly was pointing into the distance. "What is that?" She asked.

"It's a car," Gill answered, but that much was obvious.

"You think Padre sent it to pick us up? Like from the church or something?"

Gill could feel the hairs on her arms standing up. She felt less concerned about the horde of zombies at her back then the lone car in front of her. It was a small black vehicle. "No," she said in answer to the question.

"Why?" Holly asked. The car was coming right for them, as though oblivious to the oncoming horde.

"No idea," she said. "But it's definitely time to get off the road."

"But why would they be putting themselves in danger, if not to …?"

"GET OFF THE ROAD," Gill roared.

*****

"You ever use one of those things before?" Padre asked, after ending the radio conversation with Gill. He had just walked up to Lee who was sitting inside the forklift. "BOBCAT" was written across one side of the piece of equipment.

"Uh, no," Lee answered. "Got the pallet off, though." Padre looked to the far side of the Bobcat forklift. There, sprawled in a heap across the grass, was the ruined pallet of supplies.

"Nice," Padre nodded.

"I know, right?" Lee said proudly. "I'm just trying to figure out … the controls seem pretty simple. Raising and lowering the forks, check. But how do you turn this—?" The machine suddenly cut Lee off with a loud grinding of gears. Slowly at first, then gaining speed, the machine started turning. Padre stumbled backwards out of the way.

"Whoa-oh, boy. *Whoa.*" Lee shouted as the forklift started spinning in place. The thing could turn on a dime. If Padre hadn't fallen down, it's likely the forks would have knocked off his arm and a chunk of his torso, as well.

As the priest got back to his feet, he was staring in wonder at the spinning machine. Slowly, and with more grinding of gears, Lee was able to put the Bobcat back in line. After a couple more minutes, he was driving it across and around the concrete patio which marked the school's main entrance. It was full of benches. It would have been where the buses and the parents dropped off and picked up the kids. Lee was soon weaving in and out of the benches with ease.

After a couple minutes, Lee pulled the Bobcat alongside Padre. The priest was still smiling in wonder at the thing.

"Ol' hoss is pretty sweet once you break her in," Lee said.

"Do you realize what you've got there?" Padre asked. "That spinning thing you did … you could take down a dozen at a time."

"That's what I'm saying," Lee said excitedly. "I'll set this thing in front of the horde and you park behind me, mopping up what gets past me with a rifle from that turret."

"Get that thing into the roadway. I'll get out there and lead 'em to you. They can't be that far away. It's been less than a half hour."

"Hurry," Lee said. "You need to draw 'em away from the girls. I'll be ready. Just make sure I can stay on a paved surface."

*****

Gill and Holly had dashed off the road. They reached the side of a red brick house and looked back to the roadway. The black car had pulled into the driveway. A couple men both armed exited from the backseat, just as the horde was starting to spill over the roadway and across the ditch.

"Run," Gill whispered. "Over the levee."

The car screeched its tires along the pavement as it reversed back onto the road. The rear wheel drive lurched over a couple knocked-over zombies. The wheels were wrapped in snow chains. One back wheel lost traction as it collapsed into the rib cage of one of the zombies the car had bowled over. The spinning tire sprayed up a rooster tail of viscera as the small car skittered in place. The car finally lurched forward as the back wheel crunched through the zombie's rib cage.

Fortunately, the house's backyard wasn't clear-cut all the way back to the levee road. There was a stand of timber that would provide the girls some cover as they ran. Gill and Holly were able to disappear into the woods by the time the two men rounded the side of the brick house. The girls listened and watched the men as they stood scanning the backyard and trying to decide which way they had gone. Holly understood now what Gill had only felt before. These men were not here to help them. On top of that, they were really well armed. The girls watched the horde, too, as it swelled in size behind their pursuers. The horde began forking around the small house like a slow-moving wall of water. The men seemed oblivious to the danger and the moans now being directed at them.

The sound of the horde was deafening as hundreds and hundreds of voices moaned together in anticipation. Gill and Holly dashed through the small copse of woods without caring about the racket they were making. Holly's glasses nearly fell off a half dozen times as the branches whipped against her face.

"Hey, yo, Padre," Gill whispered into the radio before slipping over the crest of the levee. She was gulping down air after charging up the gentle sloping hill. It was the adrenaline. "That creep car. Bad hombres chasing us. Trying to get back your way. Going stealth. Don't call us, we'll call you. Over and out."

Holly wasn't far behind Gill, though she was breathing much heavier. When she saw that Gill had paused on the far side of the levee, she let herself collapse into the grass. She lay there panting.

"Come on," Gill began kicking Holly into motion. "Just cleared the woods. Headed this way." She took one last peak over the crest of the levee at their pursuers. They were looking up and down the wide-open stretch of the levee road, deciding which way to go. She knew they were about to see their fresh, muddy footprints leading across the roadway. She cursed, scolding herself for not being better at this. She was used to the dead chasing her, not the living. But she was going to learn from this lesson, she told herself.

As she had expected, one of the men was pointing out their tracks to the other man. Both of them had dark hair and pale skin. As the men's gaze crept up the levee, the horde of dead began breaking through the trees behind them. At first, there were no zombies. Then, there were a few, then hundreds. There were now lines of them issuing from between the trees and thickets, like strings of cheese through a grater.

"Come *on,*" Gill said tugging at Holly's foot. "We'll lose 'em in the water."

"In the *water?*" Holly nearly screamed, but it didn't matter. The sounds of the oncoming horde were echoing between the trees and the levee. "The current will suck us in ... and there're *sharks* in there."

"Sharks back that way, too," Gill answered. "We'll stick to the shallows. Hopefully, they'll divide up, maybe even ruin their guns in the mud." They trudged down the back side of the levee into a heavily wooded area. It was dark beneath the canopy of the trees. There was standing water at the foot of the trees. Dark islands of land rose here and there, they could see, deeper into the swamp.

"Gators, too," Holly continued her rant after they had dropped back into the shadows. "They find cows by the shallows, you know ..."

"Go *that* way," Gill said, pushing the other girl into the water in the downstream direction, back towards the school. "I'll join back up with you in a sec."

"... they find the cows ..." Holly was saying, as Gill disappeared into the shadows in the opposite direction. She started hustling deeper into the woods, as she saw the two men silhouetted against the top of the levee. There would soon be many more silhouettes standing against the gray overcast sky as the horde began cresting the levee.

"... they find the cows, Gill, with their legs torn clean *off,*" Holly continued ranting as Gill returned to her side a few minutes later. "What was that all about?" Holly asked. They were maybe forty or fifty yards deep into shadows of the swamp.

"I wanted them to see my footprints going upstream and yours going downstream," Gill whispered. "Maybe they'll divide up, thinking we divided up, and then it'll be two on one. Come on," Gill said, leading the girl on deeper into the forest.

Gill was making sure she kept the line of light that marked the forest's edge at her right. She didn't want to lose track of it as they pushed deeper into the forest. The held each other's hands as they trudged through the slippery mud. Luckily, only one seemed to lose her balance at a time. Holly's Converse All-Stars clung to her feet, while Gill's slip-on boots soon filled with the dark water. After another twenty yards, she lost the boots entirely to the mud's suction.

Suddenly, Gill disappeared. She had put her foot down at the edge of a hole and slipped the rest of the way. She flailed her arms and legs around until she found purchase. She crawled back over the edge of the hole and pushed her head up through the remaining foot or so of water. She scrambled away from the hole, like it had been the mouth of some giant fish. She spat out the dark water and wiped the hair from her face.

"The *hell?*" Gill finally said, still looking wild-eyed at Holly, who was trying to walk around the place where Gill had suddenly disappeared.

"Let's start walking single-file, kay?" Holly said. "Could've been a gator in that hole. Could've been a wide-open mouth waiting to *snap,*" she said clapping her hands together like a mouth.

They trudged through the mud in single-file for another thirty minutes or so before stopping to rest on one of the patches of land that rose above the water level. "Think we've gone far enough?" Holly asked. "We've had to be going now as far as we walked, right?"

"I don't know," Gill answered.

"Let's at least peak over the levee. I mean, *listen.* Do you hear anything following us? Even the sounds of the zees splashing around are dying off."

"'Dying off,' huh?" Gill said with a smirk. "Little late for that."

"*Come on,*" Holly said now beginning to pull on Gill. "Time we got out of these stupid, dark, monster-infested waters."

Gill allowed the younger girl to pull her to the verge of the forest, where they could observe their side of the levee from the shadows. They stood quietly together on the far side of a thick cypress tree.

"See?" Holly said. "Nada, nothing, not even those zeeks."

"Okay," Gill said. "See that bit of scrub up there? Get to the far side of it. We'll take cover before rolling down the other side like those two idiots from the *Princess Bride.*"

It should have been an easy slope. Between Holly's mounting exhaustion and Gill's loss of shoes, they each slipped once or twice. Gill normally looked so graceful, but just now they looked pathetic.

"Let's just not talk about that last bit when we get back home, okay?" Gill whispered, as she looked back the way they came. She didn't see any sign of their pursuers either in the forest or along the hill before it. She crept around to the far side of the small stand of trees. She saw now that it was what remained of a wide tree stump. Grass and weeds had grown up around it. The tree itself had sent up shoots which were growing into trees in their own right.

She cursed. "Where the'ell those frickers go?"

"Look," Holly said. She was looking in the opposite direction as Gill, further downstream along the levee. "The school. You can just see it around the bend."

Gill paused, finally listening to what the other girl was saying. She forcibly raised her gaze from the road and the soft grass and earth that ran along either side of it. She saw that Holly was right. The school was within sight. They top of the levee afforded a great view of the countryside downstream from them. There was a wall of trees along the far side of the roadway, but this abruptly ended in an open field. It was the same field that they had first run across trying to lead the horde away.

S. L. Smith

"It looks empty," Holly said. "No zeeks."
"Yeah," Gill said. "But no Hummer, no Padre, either."

# CHAPTER NINE:

# THE BOBCAT

Lee was nervously checking the fuel gauge of the Bobcat. His hands were sweating as he gripped the two joystick-like hand controls at his left and right knees. The grey vinyl controls were growing sticky. Most of the interior of the forklift was well-worn and coated in residue of chewing tobacco and energy drinks. He had wiped a fair bit of the plastic surfaces clean as he waited for the oncoming horde. He had over a half tank of fuel, but not much more.

When he first heard the horn of the Humvee in the distance, the forklift's cockpit suddenly felt very small. Within a foot or two of either side of his head was plexiglass and a metal cage. The walls would hold back the zombies, but they'd still be face to face, as their rotting flesh pressed and smeared across the plexiglass.

It was the front of the bobcat that sent chills back and forth across his shoulders. The front of the cockpit was a just a plexiglass door. There were no metal bars reinforcing the plastic. The door wasn't to the side of the driver's seat like a car. The door was directly in front of the driver's seat, as were the twin forks of the machine. The door would be a tough entry point for the zombies, as it was directly behind the tines of the forklift. *It's just a flimsy sheet of plastic,* Lee thought, trying to repress the thought. *There'll be nowhere to hide inside this thing if I stop moving.*

Padre nodded at him as he drove slowly past and took up a position behind the much smaller vehicle, as they had planned. Lee wondered at Padre's hand sign. He wasn't waving at him. *Did that priest just flip me off?* He would later learn that Padre had flashed him a chi-rho, by folding his thumb across his last two fingers.

He wasn't thinking about Padre's hands for long. The leading front of the horde was close at the Humvee's heels, due the priest's uncommon level of patience. Lee wanted to keep the crowd around him thin. "Charge," Lee said to himself, as he pushed the hand controls forward dramatically. There was no lurch of speed, however, to match the man's dramatic flourish. The machine plodded slowly forward at a maximum speed of less than ten miles per hour. It would be enough to outdistance himself from zombies, if necessary. He hoped.

He aimed the forklift at a quartet of angry zombies. He stopped before them as another ten or more approached from the sides. As they staggered towards the tines of the upraised fork, Lee pushed jerked the joystick to left. The bobcat started turning. By the time it had rotated ninety degrees, it was *moving*. By the time it had completed a full three-hundred-sixty-degree turn, the first quartet of zombies had dragged themselves to the place where the tines of the fork had been a moment ago. The kill zone.

Lee had just guesstimated what height to set the fork at. He had been spot on, though. The tines of the forklift swung back around with terrific speed and violence. Three heads rocketed towards left field. "A *triple*," Lee roared in bloodlust. The third zombie of the quartet had been shorter than the others, but he, too, had been eliminated. Lee didn't see exactly what happened, but its skull had caved in on impact.

The second time around, there were two packs of zombies approaching from either side. Lee had been worrying all along that more zombies would slow down the Bobcat's rotational speed. It didn't. Not yet, anyway. The tines of the fork, though they seemed blunt, cut like the Grim Reaper's sickle. It didn't always give a clean slice, like Isherwood's katanas. The machine was ruthlessly efficient, though, like the grinders had been at the gravel yard. They treated the rotted human forms like so much scrap metal, mechanically separating the brain stems from the rest of spine.

Lee stopped the Bobcat's spin on a dime. He stopped just past the zero-degree mark, twelve o'clock. He scooted the machine forward fifteen feet into the thick of the approaching crowd. The first quartet of beheaded zombies were flattened beneath the machine and gave hardly a bump in protest.

Padre had parked the Humvee and was watching the Bobcat's heavy-footed dance with concern. He had risen from the vehicle's turret and had picked off one or two strays. Only a couple had reached his vehicle, but it seemed Lee and his machine had stolen the show. The Bobcat had the full attention of the entire horde.

"Let's give the old girl a *real* test," Lee whistled from inside the forklift's cab. There were now over twenty zombies nearly within reach of the forklift when Lee started spinning. On top of that, another dozen or so would rush in before the Bobcat completed its first turn.

The Bobcat soon proved itself a cold-blooded killing machine. After its first sweep in the new position, it had been nearly perfect, but it hadn't batted a thousand. Not quite. Every zombie had been knocked off its feet, but not everyone had been put down. Lee thought he saw, though he couldn't be sure because of all the spinning, a headless woman stagger back to her feet. At the sight of her, he had felt fear as he had not felt fear since the beginning of it all.

She had been some sort of office woman, Lee thought. Her skirt had fallen off a long time ago as her waistline slowly wasted away. Maybe just enough of the brain stem was left intact, he wondered, to allow her to stagger back to her feet. He didn't see her again after the third turn. *Maybe she just collapsed.*

Padre watched from the Humvee as heads were being launched off the roadway in every direction. It was like watching a sprinkler, he thought. Padre got distracted watching as one head tumbled and bounced a good fifty feet into the field beside the school. *A grounder to right field*, he mused.

Lee rolled the Bobcat back seven feet or so. He had quickly realized that he needed to keep moving. If he didn't, he wasn't sure how the forklift would manage up a hill of body parts. He knew this kind of forklift could handle more than just the floor of a warehouse, but he didn't want to push it. He might be able to push his way through, but he might, just as likely, become immobilized.

Padre quickly realized this wrinkle in the plan, as well. He wasn't going to be able to keep moving back and forth between the turret and the driver's seat. He wasn't doing much at the moment, anyway, and took the opportunity to reposition his vehicle out of Lee's way. He turned the Humvee broadside, so he could stay in the driver's seat and still shoot from the driver's side window. He could use the window sill as a rest for his rifle. Not that it really matters, he thought. *Not much company coming my way.* The only clean-up duty he would be needed for, he mused, were all the zombie parts left in the roadway.

A sharp report from a rifle momentarily overcame the steady thumping and clacking of the forklift against skulls and spines. There was a soft, unheard *thwack* of impact, and a gray-haired skull suddenly deformed. The skull had belonged to a maimed zombie that was dragging itself slowly towards the Humvee. It had been Padre's .44 magnum Henry rifle. Padre quickly ratcheted the lever-arm and ejected the spent cartridge. The priest hated the "draggers," as they had taken to calling them. They could be the most dangerous now that it seemed like stands of tall grass and weeds were growing everywhere. Adults could wear tall boots to protect themselves, but the draggers were lethal to the children. The St. Mary's group hadn't lost any children like this, but they had just taken on a small band of survivors who had.

Lee, meanwhile, was growing more and more confident in his machine. If nothing else, the swinging fork was doing a fine job knocking the zombies away from him. But the forklift *was* doing something else, it was tearing the zombies apart. More than that, it wasn't just a bunch of animated torsos crawling about. The fork was the equivalent of a lawnmower blade, mowing down the zombies like individual blades of grass and leaving behind a perfectly clipped lawn of headless, or headless *enough*, zombies.

Lee again checked the fuel gauge. The needle had barely moved, but it had still moved. *Maybe just a sixteenth of a tank*, he thought. At this rate, he could go for another forty-five minutes. Lee cussed. Looking into the distance at the road ahead, he would need another hour, at least.

After trying to focus on the fuel gauge for a moment, Lee gulped. It wasn't out of fear for the massive amount of zombies that lay ahead of him. It was the *spinning*. He was extremely grateful for the slow retreat he had started after every five or six turns. Not because he wasn't stuck, but because it gave him a short respite from all the spinning. The constant spinning was making him nauseous. He hadn't thought about this part. He had never spent much time on boats, much less the open sea. Had he, he would have learned about his susceptibility for seasickness. An hour of nearly endless spinning now stretched out like a nightmare before him.

Something suddenly rumbled inside Lee's belly. He shivered. A moment later, the contents of his stomach were swirling around the inside of the Bobcat and splattering the inside of the plexi-glass. The caustic juices burned the inside of his mouth and throat. He winced as he felt a sudden drop in his blood pressure. He wavered near the edge of fainting. He closed his eyes and willed himself back to livid consciousness.

After the rush of vomiting, he relaxed visibly. Lee realized it had given him relief for the job ahead. He actually felt much better. The nausea from the near constant spinning had receded to manageable levels. There was, however, a new wave of nausea as he noticed the smell. It wasn't just the vomit. It was the blend of smells: the sweet smells of rotting flesh and vomit. "God help me," Lee said aloud as his eyes rolled back in his head.

Lee's head lurched back forward suddenly as he dry-heaved between his legs. He had mercifully stopped spinning for the moment and was edging several feet backwards. He reached down deep within himself to start spinning again, deeper than he had ever attempted. When he started spinning again, there was something strange in the air. There was still the sweetness, but it was a living sweetness.

"Roses," he said, shivering for a third time. The smell didn't last long, but it was long enough. The other smells and spinning had grown suddenly much more manageable. There was a glint of light. His eyes slowly focused on the right tine of the forklift, which lay ahead of him. He had, without making a conscious decision to do it, started spinning the Bobcat to his right. There was something hanging from the flat metal bar of the right tine. It was a silver chain. It was glinting and fluttering upward as it clung to the spinning forklift.

Lee laughed as he saw what was attached to the silver chain. It was a cross – *No,* he thought, a crucifix.

After a short spin, he stopped the Bobcat and reversed an extra twenty feet down the roadway, even with Padre's Humvee. "Cover me," he called over to the priest, as he flung the door of the Bobcat open. He jumped between the tines of the fork and onto the asphalt roadway. As a precaution, he had removed a pistol from one of his underarm holsters. He slid the silver chain and cross into his free hand, knocking off chunks of meat and congealed blood as he did so.

Padre was eager for the change of pace and went about his task without a word. The priest's arm and the rifle's lever moved together fluidly. It required the use of a precious resource, bullets, but the rifle was another efficient machine to clear away the zombies. Zombies seems to drop two and three at time as Padre swung into action.

It didn't take long from Lee to remove the chain and drop it around his head. He was back in the saddle just in time for when Padre needed to move farther down the road. The horde had shifted toward its new target and was beginning to grow thick around the Humvee.

Lee raised the fork back to neck height and rolled the Bobcat into the oncoming horde. Still spinning toward his right, the Bobcat seemed to grow even more efficient.

Two heads clanged against the side of the Humvee and Padre re-parked it down the road apiece. After the flurry of rifle fire covering Lee, he didn't to fire another shot. Over the course of the next *two* hours, they reversed foot by foot way past the school. When they could again see sunlight breaking through the dense horde, they were nearly back to the airport and the gas station.

Lee didn't need to turn the forklift's motor off when it was all over. The motor just sputtered off on its own. The Bobcat's fuel gauge had long since hit the zero mark. The Bobcat was completely coated in a deep red scum. When Lee finally kicked the door back open, the swinging door launched a bucketful of gore into the air. It was just a drop in the bucket, however, compared to what lay across the roadway. The black asphalt of the roadway was barely even visible. The Bobcat looked like a clot of blood along a massive spliced artery. The road stretched back to the horizon as one long swath of human wreckage.

After kicking the door open, Lee slowly rose from inside the cockpit. His knees creaked audibly. Padre was leaning against the outside the Humvee, waiting for him with one rifle still unslung. "Man," was all Lee could say as he stood stretching and looking back down the roadway. Padre, never much one for words, just nodded in appreciation.

Lee started scanning the area now that he had an unobstructed view of the fields surrounding the roadway. He looked at Padre in panic. "Where …? You haven't seen the girls?"

Padre shook his head grimly. He told the other man about the last time the girls had checked in, when Gill said don't radio them. "She had said they were going dark, into 'stealth mode,' she said. And something about some 'bad hombres' following them.

"That's it?" Lee suddenly regained his nervous energy. He began chirping incessantly with questions.

"Nothing more on the radio, either."

# CHAPTER TEN:

# PURSUIT

"Come on," Holly said tugging at Gill's arm. "Let's get back to the other road. Padre and Lee gotta be over there, right?"

Gill wasn't moving. She had felt a sudden foreboding at seeing the school in the distance. "*Shhh*, just listen," she said. She was having difficulty focusing due to a sudden pounding in her head.

Holly shifted back and forth on her feet. She was willing herself to keep quiet despite the pounding in her chest. She tried breathing softly, but found that she was having difficulty catching her breath. Her heart was beating faster. Her fear was mounting. She felt relief as Gill finally broke off toward the ditch on the far side of the levee road. Gill dropped down and just lay on the cool grass there for what seemed like an eternity.

Holly suddenly grabbed at her glasses. They had been fogging up as they ran around. She wiped the moisture away with a piece of her shirt. She hated the way she sweat in all this humidity. She looked down at herself and wished she was in better shape. She sat wondering why the apocalypse, with all its starving and running, running and starving, had not yet given her the body she always wanted. But she could fight. That was something, she thought, something that was about to be again put to the test.

Gill suddenly rocked back onto her heels. Her back had stiffened at a sound that Holly couldn't hear. Gill looked back up the roadway to the school and then hunched back down, cursing under her breath. She grabbed Holly's hand. "Come on, we'll run for the road."

"The road?" Holly whispered. "The road's right here," she said cocking her head behind them.

"No, the first road, stupid. The highway."

"Why not the *school?*"

"They're close, very close. *Too* close. We'd never make it in the open like that."

Holly nodded grimly, knowing that she wasn't about to win any foot races. "Let's fight these guys, Gill. There's only *two.*"

Gill shook her head. "They've got us outgunned, probably outnumbered, too. But be ready. We'll probably be fighting either way."

Holly nodded and heaved herself up and into a crouch. Gill closed her eyes one last time to listen. She then leaned just a bit towards the roadway. She checked both directions before leaping in the opposite direction, across the ditch and into the woods beyond. The thin woods ran along the edge of the field and eventually to the highway maybe five hundred yards on the far side.

Holly twitched at the suddenness of Gill's movements. She moved like some kind of small animal that had been startled back into hiding. Though quick at the other girl's heels, Holly didn't slice through the woods and brush nearly as quietly. Nevertheless, Holly could now hear the sounds of their pursuers. There was something crashing through the woods after them. It was living, too, Holly knew. The dead didn't move so fast.

They sounded *so* close, Holly thought with rising panic. She could almost feel hands closing around her arm or neck or ankle. *Why don't they yell out? Tell us to stop or they'll shoot?* Holly quickly decided she didn't care. Her lungs were already starting to burn with the exertion.

Gill, Holly noticed, was running through the woods holding her bo staff in one hand. She was slicing through the smaller vines that criss-crossed their path like a thick spider webs. Holly decided that now was not the appropriate time to break the rules laid down in kindergarten. She would not be running with her knives drawn.

Moments later, Gill whipped her head back to check behind her. She realized that Holly was no longer back there. She saw the younger girl's shadow not far off. The light was starting to break through the woods as they were nearing the far side.

Her eyes were adjusting to the light. The slim line of the road was emerging through the trees. She had been expecting to see the Humvee as soon as the road appeared. She hadn't realized until that moment that she had pinned all her hopes on the Humvee being there. She suddenly felt very foolish. It was as if she'd expected Padre to be waiting for them with arms open and guns blazing.

Gill could hear their pursuers crashing through the woods behind them. Nevertheless, when she finally emerged from the woods, she slowed and stopped. Holly kept running and ran right past her. She cast a look of bewilderment in Gill's direction, and kept running.

Her red hair swung back and forth as she searched up and down the road for Padre and Lee. The Humvee was nowhere to be seen. There was something that looked like a forklift down the way, but she dismissed it without another thought. She decided at that moment that they would need to stand and fight. Any second now, the men would burst from the tree line and out into the open. With Holly still running, Gill thought, she could be just the diversion she needed.

Gill fell back against a tree. She stood just inside the shadows behind the tree line. She held her bo vertically to conceal it along the shadow of the tree. She was readying herself to bring it down hard against anyone passing within range. She listened as their pursuers closed in on them. Both of the men were making plenty of noise. Gill could hear them perfectly now that she was still and forcibly slowing down her breathing. One was coming near. She could tell now that they each had their own pursuer. She could hear Holly's, as well as her own. She wondered if hers would come near enough. She would be swinging blindly, or mostly blind. There were vines everywhere. She hoped that the path of her staff would be clear.

He was within feet now. She turned and swung in one fluid movement. Their eyes locked for the thinnest slice of a moment. She saw the rage in his eyes. The emotion she saw there wasn't a reaction to her ambush, it was just there. Like rage was etched inside him.

The crack of her bo staff making impact was the next thing she knew. The staff had slid up the side of his neck along his carotid and had kept going. It went much too far up the neck. It went past the place where a small nerve, a pressure point, curled out midway along the jawbone. The jawbone should have stopped the staff from going further. The momentum of the impact should have knocked the man sideways, but it didn't. Not exactly.

Gill looked away from him sharply. Whether it was the spray of bullets erupting from the man's automatic gun or the sight of her bo staff somehow lodged in his face, she didn't know. The end of her bo staff had broken clean through the man's jaw bone. He looked on in agony as the long stick protruded from his sinus cavity, somewhere deep within his cheekbone. Even then, as the life drained from his eyes, the rage remained.

The red hair jumped from one shoulder to the other, as she heard a squeal of fear not far away. It was Holly. Between this and the horrific scene she had just caused, she didn't notice the soft fall of the radio into the wet mud at her feet.

Gill watched as Holly's pursuer locked one arm around her neck. Holly's screaming suddenly stopped as it lodged in her throat.

Gill's heart jumped with a mixture of hope and fear. She turned back to the dying man, hoping it wasn't too late. She crawled over to his where he lay. He was beginning to seize. Her bo had notched something critical deep inside the man's skull. She lunged for the automatic rifle still slung across his shoulder. Her movements were wild, though, and grasping.

"That's *enough*," a male voice said behind her. Gill stopped. She had dropped her staff as she lunged for the gun. Not only that, the rifle was still tangled around the man's arm. As he thrashed about in his death convulsions, the dying man had unwittingly tricked and disarmed her.

Still, it wasn't enough to stop the berserking redhead. She uncoiled her body and made to strike. She would launch herself against the last pursuer head on. But he was too far. She soon stilled, as he sent a spray of bullets whizzing past her body and into the soft earth beyond. Gill had become a skilled fighter over the last few weeks, since the apocalypse began, but she was not accustomed to being shot at. Zombies didn't shoot back.

If the last man had been just a little closer, or if she hadn't dropped her bo, or if she hadn't hit that guy so hard, or if Holly had just struggled a little more, or if the dead man's rifle had just come free – these would be the questions that would haunt her over the coming days. In the end, she would realize that she had just lost her nerve in the last, critical moment. She hadn't been prepared for the moment. She had grown too accustomed to fighting zombies. She had been outmaneuvered and would pay a terrible price for it, but she would never let it happen again.

The man staring back at her was still holding Holly around her neck. The girl was still squirming, but her eyes were now lolling back in her head. In another moment, Holly's body fell slack as she passed out. He let her fall, crumpling into a heap on the ground. All the while, his cold, predatorial eyes never left Gill's face. Gill couldn't tell if he was one of the first two guys that had climbed out of the car or not. They all had the same look. She cursed at herself for being so completely beaten.

He was pale, Gill saw. His hair fell down to his shoulders in dark, greasy clumps. His eyes were just small points of light. She couldn't tell, in the half-light of the trees and brush, whether there were whites to his eyes at all. She knew instantly that he reminded her of a rat. His nose didn't help. It was more like a flaccid, pale snout. "Rat man" would be her name for him always, no matter what she later learned.

Soon, both of the girls were unconscious. Their next memories would be of flitting in and out of consciousness and of traveling by boat along the river.

*****

"You mean they're just *gone*? Just poof. Nothing?" Lee was peppering Padre incessantly with unhelpful and repetitious questions from the passenger's seat of the Humvee. It was as if Lee's internal monologue switch had been snapped clean off.

"Not *nothing*," Padre said growing irritated. "She said 'bad hombres'."

Padre had been in constant radio contact with Isherwood and St. Mary's during the lulls of their battle with the double horde, that is, the combined hordes from inside the school and around the airport fence. Isherwood had created a secondary defensive line back at the gas station. His precautions, though, had proven unnecessary following Lee's heroics with Bobcat. Isherwood had posted five rifles across the highway, but these would be quickly converted into search parties now that the threat had been eliminated.

Chet had been keeping an ear to the radio transmissions all along, not straying far from Isherwood's side. He was a fool, Chet had thought, to let himself be parted from Gill in the first place. She had kissed him. He had thought it would never happen, but it did. Afterwards, he had wanted her to have her space, not wanting to scare her off. She was so fiercely independent. And now, she might be gone forever or worse.

Isherwood wouldn't have been able to hold Chet back, even if he'd wanted to. Chet was off in a dead sprint towards the levee as soon as Padre had passed on the message about 'bad hombres'. Padre hadn't passed on the message immediately, though. It was an oversight that he'd soon learn to regret.

Isherwood had called out for Justin to follow Chet, but Justin was already jumping in his Escalade. Isherwood's party had watched Justin catch up with Chet along the Airport Road, but hadn't heard from them since.

Isherwood was just finishing catching Padre up all this over the radio. Throughout it all, Lee was still muttering to himself off and on.

"Glenn is coming now from St. Mary's," Padre interrupted Lee's ramblings. "He'll be able to track the girls. The dirt is soft enough."

"Keep driving. Don't just give up," Lee said.

Padre dismissed the comment as irrelevant. Lee had just performed what amounted to a miracle, Padre thought. He had killed thousands of zombies, possibly, and with just a forklift, but he clearly needed time to decompress afterwards. Despite some efforts at charity, Padre had begun using the military vehicle's horn to interrupt Lee's ramblings. The horn didn't seem to matter, either to Lee or to their safety. The place had been nearly perfectly emptied of zombies. Before joining back up with what was left of Isherwood's group, they would make three circuits back and forth between the airport and St. Anne's church in Morganza and along both the highway and the river road. Through all of this, there had been little to no sign of leftover zombies, despite Padre hammering on the horn, and none at all of the girls.

# CHAPTER ELEVEN:

# CROSSROADS

Isherwood held his small group back at the gas station as he waited for Glenn to join them. There were now only two others, besides Isherwood, now that Chet and Justin had left them. These were Patrick and Wilson. Wilson had really just come along for the target practice. He was only a novice with a rifle and still kept his trust makeshift spear near at hand.

Patrick called out that Padre's Humvee was approaching. Near about that same time, Isherwood heard the first rumblings of Glenn's diesel truck approaching. Once his strength had returned, Sara's dad had been quick to visit Lieux Chevrolet and go truck-shopping. When the truck finally came into view, Isherwood was relieved to see Sara's brothers, Micha and Eli, riding in the cab with Glenn. He saw that his father-in-law had picked out for his new truck one that was nearly identical to his old truck: a silver Dodge Ram.

"So where should we start?" Micha asked the gathering of older men. The boy's voice was just a little too excited, given the circumstances. Isherwood and Glenn exchanged glances, smirking at each other, before turning to Padre. Padre, for his part, looked briefly at Lee. Lee was standing beside him, but staring off into the distance. Staring without seeing, Padre observed.

"It's hard to say," Padre began. "There was a zombie up the road apiece. Something had driven through its rib cage. There were tire tracks still in it and leading away from it. Smallish car from the look of it. That's likely what the 'bad hombres' got out of. There might be a trail of viscera leading away from it, if we're lucky."

"You're saying some of the 'bad hombres' got out of the car and started after the girls from there?" Glenn asked.

"Yeah, there was a driveway. Most of those houses just have a gravel drive, but this one had a concrete-looking drive. It was in front of a brick house. Nothing special. You'll see it. Only ..."

"Only what, Padre?" Patrick asked.

"Only I doubt there'll be much of a trail," Padre continued. "A few hundred, maybe even a thousand, feet trampled around that house from the look of it. They eventually all came back our way, but not before flattening every bush and blade of grass around that house first."

"Wait," Micha asked. "That doesn't make sense. The bad guys drove their car after the girls? Through the yard?"

"No, son," Glenn said impatiently. "Padre's saying the car dropped off a couple guys. The guys started chasing the girls on foot. The car stayed on the roads, probably taking the long way to meet back up with the guys on foot, you know? That's what you're saying, right?"

Padre was nodding, clearly impressed. "Yeah, but I think you've already passed me up."

"So two trails, huh?" Isherwood asked. "Plus whatever Chet and Justin manage to find, assuming it's not trouble."

Patrick was shaking his head. "We need more people." Wilson nodded, tightening his grip on the spear.

"Look," Glenn said. "My boys and I can handle tracking both trails. Y'all try and catch up with the others."

"There's something else, too," Isherwood said, motioning behind him with his thumb. "That airport. Something inside had been steadily drawing the zeeks to it. I don't like not knowing what it was. And I *definitely* don't like putting whatever it is between us and St. Mary's. We've pretty much left the church without any men to defend it, just the Amazons. Who knows? Whoever took the girls might not be alone. This might all be part of a larger strategy to lure us away from the church."

Micha cursed under his breath. His father shot him a smoldering look in reply. Eli even jumped a little.

The others were quiet for a time mulling over Isherwood's insights. Padre was standing with his arms crossed tightly across his chest and staring down at the ground. Lee was still just staring.

"Well, look," Glenn said. "We can only do what we can do. Me and my boys will start trying to pick up the two trails. And, Padre ..."

"Lee and I will go try and find Chet and Justin." Padre answered. "They've got a radio, right?"

"Right," Isherwood answered. "And I'll go check out the airport."

"I'll go with 'ya," Patrick said. "None of us should be out alone right now. Eyes on every back."

"Couldn't agree more," Isherwood answered. He was glad for the company. "Wilson? How about you stick with Padre? I've gotta bad feeling about what those guys are walking into. In fact, if all goes well at the airport – if it's just a radio or something, you know, that never went off – we'll be headed your way, too. Everybody check in every half hour, okay? If you gotta go quiet for a while just switch to channel four, okay? Don't turn your radio off."

Before they separated into three groups, Glenn asked Padre to give them all a blessing. Wilson joined Padre and Lee in the Humvee, and they were soon gone. The blessing inspired Isherwood with one last idea before leaving the little defensive line they had thrown together. With Glenn driving his own vehicle, either Isherwood or Patrick would need to leave their truck behind. Before they left Patrick's truck behind, Isherwood realigned it to block the roadway. Apart from the River Road, it was the only way into town from this direction. He also rigged up Patrick's CB radio, so it would chirp at them if somebody opened the driver's side door.

Patrick was giving Isherwood a funny look when he finally got in the driver's seat of his Jeep. "I just don't know what we're dealing with here, buddy," he told his friend. "Just trying to stay a couple steps ahead."

"Like I always say," Patrick nodded. "Better ahead than dead."

*****

"Can't you just plow through the fence or something?" Chet was asking. He had jumped in the passenger seat of Justin's vehicle willingly enough when Justin had caught up with him, but he had been chomping at the bit ever since.

"There'll be a gate or something soon enough," Justin said. "Don't worry, man."

"And if it's locked?" Chet asked indignantly. "We'll just have to plow through it, too, right? *Right?*"

"Look, man. Just up 'head. There's a nice open gate and a road for us to get up and on the levee."

"'bout time! We've been driving all this time in the opposite direction."

"How'd'you know it's the opposite direction?"

"Because, man – they'll couldn't've got past the school on foot."

"Okay, that sounds right and all, but how'd you put all that together? You'd never even heard of Morganza a couple days ago."

"I don't know," Chet said, as though his brain had suddenly fogged up. "I just have a picture in my head."

Justin wrinkled his eyebrows at this and started observing the younger man out of the corner of his eye from then on. "Okay. Whatever that means. So what's this picture telling you?"

"Turn left, once you get atop the levee."

"Right, picture in *my* head was telling me that much, too."

81

"Yeah, so, after that, we'll drive a little bit. We'll see the school out to our left. Pretty much right when we see the school, we'll need to get off the road. I mean, go on foot. I'm thinking they'll be on the riverbank at about that point. Don't know if they'll still be there, though."

"You know the riverbank's not just right on the other side of the levee, right? That could be a pretty hard slog through man-eating mud, you know."

"No, I don't think it will be."

"The picture again, huh?" Justin's eye-rolling was nearly audible at this point.

"Uh-huh."

******

Despite Justin's skepticism, it had been exactly as Chet had pictured it. Cutting through the swampy woods on the far side of the levee, there was a long line of half-sunken timber mats that disappeared into the woods.

The sun was sinking low in the sky as the Escalade crunched to a stop along the gravel road atop the levee. "So if that's the school," Chet was saying with his eyes closed. "Then, the road ought to be ..."

Justin watched as the other man's index finger slowly gravitated toward a spot along the passenger window. Chet's eyes were shut tight throughout, as though opening his eyes might break the spell. When the man's finger finally stilled, Justin lurched over the vehicle's center console to see what lay below. "You've gotta be ..." he trailed off. "Like Dorothy's yellow-brick road."

Chet was already gone while Justin was still fumbling with his seatbelt. "Come on. You gotta slow down, jack." Justin was saying, but he might as well have been talking to himself. "Guess we're going on foot," he continued, now truly talking to himself. He grabbed his trusty AR-15 from behind his seat and clipped on a sidearm, as well. He grabbed a second ArmaLite for Chet, as he was pretty sure the other man had run off unarmed.

Justin locked the doors of his vehicle and slammed the door shut behind him. "You'll be safe here, old lady," he told his vehicle. "You be a big ol' bread crumb for the others." He mumbled the last part to himself as he sprinted down the gentle slope of the levee carrying the extra rifle by the barrel, while his own rifle bounced against his back.

"Dude," Justin whispered loudly as his feet banged along the slim road. "Take this from me." The road was not perfectly set into the ground. Sections of the timber mats angled sharply into the mud. In the half-light, it was impossible to tell whether it was just a puddle standing along the mat or a man-sized hole. The condition of the road forced even Chet to slow down. Otherwise, Justin might never have caught up with him.

Justin finally had to rap the end of the rifle against Chet's shoulder to get him to stop a second for the hand off. "Just throttle back a sec and think, will ya?" Justin scolded Chet. "A little teamwork and strategy might help save her life, you know. What were you gonna do without a gun, anyway, McFly? Not smart."

"If I slow down," Chet groaned. "I might lose the image in my head. It's like I'm chasing a light in the distance now, or a white rabbit. I keep losing sight of it."

"Okay, fine. Do your thing. I'll handle the plan part." Justin looked back to see if he could still see his Escalade and the top of the levee, but the trees had already closed in on them. It was growing dark fast under the canopy of trees. Even now, they could barely see fifteen feet ahead or beyond the makeshift road.

Justin gasped as Chet's foot nearly slipped off the mat. "What?" Chet asked. "So what if I get a little muddy?"

"So *that's* what," Justin said, pointing at a piece of plastic on the left side of the path, maybe ten feet back.

"What're you pointing at," Chet asked. "That bit of trash?"

"Look closer, bro." Justin watched as, despite his hurry, curiosity got the better of Chet. Slowly, Justin saw his eyes widen.

"Is that a ...?"

"Yeah, believe it."

"No way. A whole car?"

"Forget it," Justin said, prodding Chet along. "Just be careful." There had been just two plastic saucers visible along the surface of the mud. It was the grill of some kind of Jeep or utility vehicle. The mud had consumed the rest of the vehicle. It had likely run off the path, and was now being slowly digested by the swamp.

They had cleared another five or six timber mats when the woods began to fall away. The mats were nearly completely submerged now, and their legs were sinking deeper and deeper in the water with each passing yard. The dim half-light of the forest quickly gave way as the river shined in gold and silver ahead of them. Soon, they were holding their hands up against the blinding light of the setting sun reflected along the wide and churning river. Their retinas burned even when they looked straight down at their feet. It was getting harder and harder to see the mats through the water. The swamp water had turned now to river water, which was darkening even as it reflected the sunset.

"Chet!" Justin kept whispering as the younger man drew farther away from him. "Slow down, man. The current's starting to pull at my boots."

"Slow down?" Chet said, finally turning back. "Can't you hear that?"

Justin's already-squinting face grew comical as it squinted further. "Hear *what?*" He started to say, and then fell silent.

# CHAPTER TWELVE:

# DEAD AIR

Isherwood's Jeep rolled to a stop outside the large chain-link gate that led to the small administration building of the airport. Isherwood had only driven himself and Patrick a quarter of a mile from the gas station. He felt a little funny for driving a distance they could have easily walked, but the Jeep was like their mobile base. They had stocked all the vehicles with extra ammo and gun, first-aid kits, and provisions – even extra auto parts. They were ready for almost anything, they hoped.

"Nice fence," Patrick observed as he closed the passenger door softly behind him. "Bet you've had your eyes on this place for a while, eh? 'Part of a larger strategy,' 'enemies between us and the church' – whatever, amiright? You just couldn't wait any longer to get at this place."

Isherwood smirked, but couldn't help look guilty. "I'm sure we'll soon have a chance to lay down our lives for those two girls, don't you worry. It's weird, though. This place. It's got a perfect fence and all sorts of land inside for farming – and my *God*, the planes! – and it didn't even …"

"What?" Patrick said, tilting his head.

"Enter my *mind*. I completely didn't even think about this place until the other day, or did I? D'you remember?"

"I dunno. One big blur since that day you came honking by our subdivision with a town-full of zombies behind you, like the pied piper or something."

As they had been talking, Isherwood had walked over to the edge of the gate where it was joined to the rest of the fence with a chain and a Master-Lock. Patrick meanwhile had turned to face one of the last zombies still stalking around the gate. Hundreds had been lured away by Padre's crew, but there were still a few stragglers.

"This was supposed to be an easy day, you know?" Isherwood said as he tried squeezing through the space between the fence and the gate. He got one shoulder through, but his head and katana wouldn't fit. He tried putting the sword through first, but the space was still too tight for his head. He cursed. "Hate ruining a perfectly good lock, but …"

"Let's just – *hrumph!* – climb it," Patrick said as he swung his sledgehammer up and through the jaw of the zeek that had finally stumbled into range.

Isherwood looked up to the top of the fence and winced. "Razor wire?"

*Womp.* The zombie's skull caved in as Patrick brought down the sledgehammer for a double tap. "Sure," Patrick said, taking a deep breath. "We'll just throw the floormats over it. Not like we haven't done it before."

"Eh, let's just cut the lock and zip-tie it back. We can drive the Jeep inside the gate, too."

Patrick smirked at Isherwood. "Not sure if you're being lazy or smart."

"Maybe a little of both," Isherwood answered, as he walked to the back of the Jeep to grab a set of bolt-cutters.

"*Dang*," Patrick said, taking a moment to scan the whole area. "Padre and Lee really did clear out this whole area. It's so quiet and still, like the whole world is just empty. Almost prefer seeing one of things stumbling around. Kinda like *The Langoliers* or something."

"The what?" Isherwood answered absent-mindedly returning to the gate with the bolt cutters.

"It's like the world has moved on and these jerks are *slowly* digesting yesterday. Nevermind. It's a Stephen King book."

"You know, you're right."

Patrick's eyes lit up. "About us being in a Stephen King book?"

Isherwood grunted struggling with the bolt cutters. "Uh, no. About it being really quiet. We should be able to hear whatever was drawing those things over here."

"Or the noise has just stopped," Patrick snapped back. "Or it just turns on and off intermittently, or, I don't know, a thousand other reasons."

"Mood swing much?" Isherwood whispered as he struggled to pull the bolt cutters closed. He exhaled sharply suddenly as the lock's steel shackle snapped apart. "Sorry about the book, okay? I'll never make fun of Stephen King again, I promise?"

Seeing Isherwood uncoiling the chain, Patrick jumped into driver's seat of the Jeep and drove it through the gate. There was a short driveway which led to the office and the vast expanse of concrete beyond.

Isherwood rolled the gate back into place as soon as the Jeep had passed. After he had coiled the chain back around the metal posts of the gate and fence, he walked over to the Jeep to get the zip ties, half-expecting Patrick to have had them ready. He pulled on the handle of the cargo hatch and it slipped through his fingers noisily. He tapped on the back windshield, but there was no response from within, so he tapped again.

Just then, there was the creaking sound of metal as hands began to pull on the chain-link gate. The chain began to slip with the movement. "Where'd you come from?" Isherwood asked the zombie, not expecting an answer.

He walked around to the front of the Jeep and tapped on the tinted window. "Hey man, what gives? Unlock it. We're starting to get visitors back here."

The power window slid down a few inches. "Say it," Patrick said.

"I'm not gonna …"

"*Say* it."

"Are you *serious*?" Isherwood whined, but there was no response.

"Fine. 'Stephen King is the *king* of horror.' Are we good?"

"And say 'I'm sorry for having offended his highness.'"

"No way I'm saying that," Isherwood groaned, but just then the chain slipped completely off the gate and clattered to the concrete and grass.

"*Just* kidding," Patrick said as he quickly pressed unlock and jumped out to help his friend.

"No," Isherwood said. "You get the zip ties. This is a job for a lady."

Patrick shot his friend a funny look, but returned to the vehicle nonetheless. Meanwhile, Isherwood was unsheathing his sword. He set his feet and, bring his head level with the sword, thrust it through the gap between the gate and the fence. Drawing himself back up to his full height, the zombie slumped forward then back.

"Quite a dame," Patrick nodded. "Does the sword have a name?"

Isherwood shook his head, adding, "but she is a lady."

Several minutes later, with the gate secured behind them, they began searching the office building. Getting inside was easy enough. There was a bloodstain marking the place where a body had been dragged across the wooden planks of the porch which ran the length of the building. They soon realized that the body hadn't been dragged far. There was sneakered foot still propping the door open.

"I really hope there's something attached to that sneaker," Patrick moaned in dread.

"Be careful what you wish for," Isherwood answered. He moved into the guard position as Patrick slowly opened the door.

"Knock, knock," Isherwood announced, as Patrick inspected the dead body at the entrance.

"Well," Patrick mused. "There is a body attached to the foot. Sort of."

After listening and watching for any activity inside the building and seeing none, Isherwood dropped his gaze to the body. "Nice. I'll be keeping my out for the rest of him."

The entire torso of the corpse was missing. The pants were tousled, but facing upward. Only the lumbar section of the man's spine remained. The pants had begun collapsing inward due to rot and the removal of much of the man's waistline. "It's actually pretty lucky that the dead heads left us with this half," Patrick was saying, as he searched the pockets of the work pants. "Because *look*."

As Isherwood watched, something came jangling out of the man's pocket. "Gotta be kidding me! That's almost too lucky."

"Lucky we don't have to depend on your lock-'Smithing' skills, you mean."

Isherwood groaned in response. "You'd think I'd have more natural ability given my name."

"Still better than me, Ish. There any reason this place would have guns and ammo? I mean, what sort of 'high dollar' supplies does a place like this have?"

"Radio equipment for one. Don't think we'll see guns and ammo." They divided up searching either side of the main room of the building. It was a large room with an open floorplan. It had a large sitting area on one side and a workspace on the other. There was a wall of windows on the far side of the room and another porch beyond. Something or someone had crashed through one of the windows on this side. Doors led out of the main room toward either side of the building.

"I'm kinda doubting we'll see people. *Live* people, either. You'd think if there were any survivors, they wouldn't still be using 'Legs' over there as a doorstop."

"Did you happen to notice if this building had antennas on top?" Isherwood asked.

"Nah, just a wind sock, maybe." As Isherwood rummaged through desk drawers and cabinets behind him, Patrick stood looking out the windows at the back of the building. "*That's* probably where we ought to be heading."

"Yup," Isherwood said, coming to stand beside Patrick. "That'll be the place." In the distance, somewhere at the center of the airstrip that ran the length of the fenced-in area, there was two-story building with an antenna tower array rising from it. "Place is probably too small for its own air traffic control tower." Isherwood bent his head down to walk through what remained of the broken window.

"Dude," Patrick said. "Let's just drive over there."

Isherwood laughed. "Oh, *sure*, get all sassy just because your idea's clearly better."

\*\*\*\*\*\*

"You sure you want to announce our arrival out here all out in the open?" Patrick asked from the passenger seat of the Jeep.

"Worried about a sniper?" Isherwood asked.

"Yeah, but I guess you'll say, not much we can do about that."

"If somebody was gonna do us like that, I'd think they'd already've done it. We were pretty much sitting ducks back at the gate. Besides, the 'bad hombres', if they're here, seem to have a kidnapping M.O."

"For women, maybe."

"Okay, yeah, but even so, everybody's worth more alive than dead these days."

"Funny how things change," Patrick said. "Okay, let 'er rip. Guess it's best not sneaking up on people these days, anyway."

The last of Patrick's words were drowned out as Isherwood laid on the Jeep's horn. He honked in long blasts. Their group had taken to honking in short, staccato beats for emergencies, so any of their group within earshot would now that, at least for now, they were safe, as well as their location. Eventually, Isherwood thought, they'd need to develop their own distinctive beats – that, and have everybody learn Morse code or least put code cheat sheets with all the cars and radios.

Isherwood had parked the Jeep on the far side of the airstrip. From here, they had a clear view of all the buildings. They were still a couple hundred yards away from the building with the radio antennas. Even if there was a sniper, he'd have difficulty making a clean shot.

After a minute or so, a half dozen zombies had begun staggering toward them from the shadows of the empty buildings and flight hangars. There were a couple more outside the fence that had thrown their bodies against the chain-link fence.

"I got this," Isherwood said, opening the driver's door. Patrick likewise reached for his, the passenger, door handle. "*Don't* ..." Isherwood blurted out, and Patrick recoiled his hand as though he had touched something hot. Isherwood continued, "... get out of the vehicle from your side, if you can help it. You've got the main building out that way. There's a direct line of fire, if you give it to 'em. Just hunker down for a sec, okay?"

Patrick slouched down in his seat begrudgingly. "You really think there's somebody out here?"

"Eh, you're probably right," he said, opening the back door to grab a rifle. He was in the habit of tucking his katana between the driver's seat and the door, and he left the sword there for now. With a rifle in hand, he lowered himself to the concrete tarmac beside the Jeep. "But it's been a bad day. I'm just not wanting to take any more chances. Turn this day into a disaster. Help me watch my six, will ya?"

Isherwood wasn't sure if the .22LR rifle he'd grabbed would be enough to penetrate a skull, even a softened one, at this distance. He might need to let them get pretty close, he thought, within twenty or thirty yards. He felt pebbles of concrete rubbing against his shirtsleeves and pant legs as he stretched into a shooting position under the Jeep. He leaned his face across the rifle's stock and was taking a moment to scan the place through his scope.

He tested his range on the nearest zombie, which was still a hundred yards off. He fired the rifle, which, though normally pretty quiet, echoed pretty loudly across the openness of the airstrip. The zeek was nearly completely bald, another workman or mechanic, with an impressive beard that only partially concealed a gaping hole where its carotid artery had been. There wasn't much kick to the .22, so he was able to watch his bullet's progress through the scope. He actually saw the flesh of the zombie's bald pate crease as the bullet glanced off the forehead. The bone at the forehead was just too thick, Isherwood thought with irritation. He'd have to shoot through the eye socket to drop a zombie at this range, unless he wanted to waste .270 bullets and make a lot more noise.

It only took one more try for him to sink his shot, though he doubted the bullet would ever find a way out of the skull. It was enough, though. The bearded zombie staggered one more step forward, seemed to waver a moment, and then crumpled into an inanimate heap of denim.

As Isherwood waited for the rest of the approaching zombies to get within range, he scanned the buildings through his scope. Two long plane hangars stood at right angles to the airstrip on the near side of the tower. He could just see the back end of a plane sticking out between them. It looked like it had been taxing but never quite made it to its destination. He couldn't tell for sure, but he thought he saw shadows moving within. He made a mental note of the hazard, and angled his rifle back toward the steadily advancing zombies.

# CHAPTER THIRTEEN:
# RIVER RATS

Justin and Chet had arrived only seconds after the little fishing boat's motor had cranked up. There was still a puff of smoke hanging on the air. To Justin, it seemed like the boat was sitting in the middle of the river. There was just too much light reflecting off the water's surface. There was no way to see through it to the rough timber mat pier below. Nevertheless, Chet was still charging toward the little boat. He looked like he was running across a pool of molten gold. Between blinks, Justin could just make out several, maybe three or four figures silhouetted in the boat.

Chet barely altered his course, even when someone inside the boat started shooting at him. It must have been pistol fire, because the aiming was poor, that or the shooter was likewise blinded by the setting sun. Justin didn't yet have time to think about any of this as he dropped to a prone position, half-submerged in the water. He pointed his AR toward the boat and realized there was no way he would be able to return fire to the boat. He had no idea who or what he was shooting at. He sprayed the air above their heads with a quick barrage of bullets.

It did the trick. The kidnapper or kidnappers stopped firing. Instead, they angled the boat further into the river, cutting a forty-five degree angle into the current.

"Chet, get *down*," Justin yelled. He cursed. Justin was certain that he wasn't stopping until he was flinging his body into the river or getting sucked into the mud. "I've gotta shot at the motor if you just get *DOWN!*"

"'bout time," Justin whispered as Chet suddenly disappeared from view. He had, as Justin expected, slipped off a timber mat. Justin knew the young man was about to be buried alive with a lungful of mud, but he had to take the shot while he had it. He took a split second to aim and squeezed off a few rounds at the spot where the water was churning up behind the boat. The first two *thwacked* into the water, but the last one *twanged* as it hit home. He couldn't take the chance that he'd merely dented one of the motor's propeller blades, so he squeezed off another volley of shots. He aimed just the slightest bit higher. He actually saw the plastic casing of the motor fly away from the back of the boat. There was a delayed and muffled explosion and the steady humming of the motor roared suddenly in protest before grinding to a halt.

Justin threw himself back to his feet in time to see Chet's head slip below the water. He didn't have time to watch the boat slowly and awkwardly turn into the current and slip away downstream. Justin didn't understand how Chet hadn't slipped off the rickety boardwalk sooner. He fell hard once, soaking himself and filling the barrel of his gun with mud.

When he finally got to the place where Chet fell in, he was only able to find the spot because of the bubbles. He groped blindly through the water until his hand hit against something solid. He grabbed at it and pulled. His grip slipped once, but he rotated himself for better leverage and pulled once more. His muscles strained as he pulled harder and harder. The bit of Chet's arm – *God*, he hoped it was Chet's arm – came excruciatingly slow. Finally, his force overcame the mud's suction and a torso slid out as though freshly born. The excised hands groped blindly along the submerged timber mat and even Justin's face. Justin had just enough time for a wave of hot fear to pass over him, *Could he have turned that fast?*

In the time it took Justin to drag Chet's body onto the timber raft beside him, the younger man hadn't breathed once. Justin flipped him on his back. His head was covered in a thick coat of sticky mud. The water rose to the edges of his face. "Sit up, buddy," Justin said, pulling him up by grabbing handfuls of the man's shirt. Justin hit him hard against his back. Twin rivulets oozed from the corners of Chet's mouth, but there were still no signs of life. Justin let the man splash back down into the water.

Justin angled the man's head back and pinched his nose. "You've got to be kidding me," he said. "You better not come back just to eat my face." Justin bent over and pushed some air into the man's mouth. He watch out of the corner of his eye to see if Chet's chest would rise. It did, but not much. "Sit back up, buddy. Aw, Jeez, aw Jeeez."

Justin not only slapped him across the back but tried hugging him from behind and pulling his guts up and into his lungs. Vomit and mud slopped into the water. "Excellent," Justin winced and let the man fall back onto his back. He again shifted Chet's head and pinched his nose. He pushed another shot of air into the man's lungs. Chet's chest moved, really moved, this time. Justin switched over to chest compressions.

91

"*Crap,*" he said. "How many times, how hard? We remembers this stuff?" He winced again as a thought occurred to him. He started humming a song and pumping Chet's chest with the melody. "Ah, ah, ah, ah … stayin' alive. This really sucks. Ah, ah, ah, ah," he continued.

He leaned back over Chet's mouth, knowing, just knowing, that those mud and vomit-splattered teeth were about to rip off his lips. "The kiss of death, literally," he grumbled as he again pushed air into the unconscious man's chest.

Out of the corner of his eye, Justin saw the man's chest lurch and convulse. He jerked his head away, but not in time. His mouth filled with the contents of the other man's lungs and throat. Justin was still cursing and spitting it all out of his mouth, as the man rose to a sitting position behind him. "You better be alive, buddy, 'cause I'm gonna *kill'ya.*"

After his tantrum, Justin had ended up with his back to Chet. He didn't know what he was about to turn and see. Maybe the end of all things, he thought. If it came to that, he decided he'd just throw himself into the nearest mud hole.

Before he could even turn around, a hand was grabbing at his shoulder. "Where …?" He heard the thing behind him whisper. "Are they gone?"

"*Yeah,* they're gone. And you just upchucked in my *mouth. And,* you're welcome by the way."

"Where?" Chet kept saying, as he tried getting up again. He was squinting up-river.

"Come on! I just saved your idiot life," Justin fumed.

"Dude, gold star," he said, coughing up another glob of mud. "Can you … still see them?"

"Yeah, yeah, maybe. The other way. They're floating downstream. If we had a boat, we could just … *sshhh,* sshh, shhh."

Chet looked around in fear and bewilderment. The sudden head movement caused him to collapse back onto the next timber mat and vomit some more.

"*Shhh,*" Justin snapped. He had stood up and was facing upriver. "Do you hear that? Something very bad is about to happen or very good." The sound of a boat motor was growing. Another boat was coming down the river. It sounded as if it would appear around the river bend any moment. "Maybe, uh," he said, dropping down to one knee and shouldering his AR. "Maybe you should hide or something."

"Boat," Chet choked, staggering back to his feet and struggling to find the next timber mat.

"Great, you came back to life as a pirate."

\*\*\*\*\*\*

Isherwood found, as he had during previous encounters, that the .22 was really only good for headshots within fifty yards. That made it useful enough for most every situation. Once all the loose zombies had been eliminated coming from the buildings, he crawled around to the back of the Jeep. He got up on his knees and used the corner of the rear bumper as a rest. He tried aiming through the gaps of the chain-link fence, but he heard a couple bullets *ping* as they ricocheted off the fence. He would have just used his knife and stabbed at the zombies through the fence, but he was still avoiding being in the open.

"Now what?" Patrick asked when Isherwood slid back into the driver's seat.

"Well," Isherwood started. "I was hoping you'd've come up with something. Did you see any movement in the tower building?"

"Nah. I've been crouching down the whole time, mostly. Think I even nodded off."

"Dreaming about those Langoliers, weren't'ya? Hey, wasn't that dude from *Perfect Strangers* in the movie?"

"You *did* see it," Patrick swooned and then, just as quickly, deflated. "Movie sucked. Book was better. Always is."

"I figured we'd just park behind one of the metal buildings and sprint through the open places," Isherwood said, interrupting Patrick before he could get going on the subject and noting his friend's use of 'is' instead of 'was'. They had all developed ticks, Isherwood had noticed. There were certain subjects that most all of the survivors would linger over if given the chance. He thought it might be a good thing, though, maybe some kind of survival mechanism. It was like their brains were subconsciously switching to another reality, back to the way things had been. He guessed it had some kind of restorative effect, like daydreaming or even nightdreaming.

"Heck, let's just drive right up to the place," Patrick said.

"Haven't you been *listening*?" Isherwood growled. "The whole reason we're here and not there, why I shot those things on my belly under the car, et cetera, et cetera, is because this might all be a trap. Something's obviously been drawing those things *here*. Something's *here*." Isherwood's rant devolved into cursing.

Isherwood blinked suddenly like something had flown into his eye. He looked down at his hands to see them balled into fists. His fingernails were cutting into the flesh of his palms. He then looked at Patrick whose hand was on the air conditioner vent. He had angled it into Isherwood's face. "Whoa," Isherwood said, rubbing at the center of his forehead. "I sorta …"

"Blacked out for a second?" Patrick asked. "Yeah. It happens. You're metabolizing trauma and stress. It's like when you eat foreign food and your body reacts with a load of gas."

Isherwood smiled. "I was just thinking about that. I guess we all have our ticks."

"Ticks and the lyme disease to go with 'em."

"So, you wanna just drive right up, huh? I really never even thought about taking the direct approach."

"It has its advantages. A. Less walking. B. We get to stay inside the vehicle longer. And the big one. Uh, C. We don't surprise them or him. If we weren't trying to keep radio silence for the other guys, we could just radio them."

Isherwood was nodding appreciatively.

"Besides," Patrick said. "I did see one thing while you were shooting. That." Patrick pointed at the tower building.

"What?" Isherwood said leaning forward. "See what?"

"Look next to the wind sock."

"What?" There was something there, but the wind had it and he couldn't make it out. The setting sun was playing with all the shadows, too. "What is that? Some rope?"

"A noose."

******

Justin cursed. "Is that a boat or nuclear fusion sun bomb coming toward us? My retinas are on *fire*." His finger twitched at the trigger. "Should I shoot? Just a quick spray to soften them up?"

"No," Chet struggled to say. "No holes."

They would later compare the shadowy figures in the approaching boat to Washington and his soldiers crossing the Delaware. "Need a ride?" Glenn called out.

"Y'all walking on water or something?" Micha called out, as Glenn set the motor to idle. They were still another twenty yards away.

"Pull up the motor, Eli," Glenn said. "Can y'all get any closer? Or's that it?" The boat had a flat bottom. Before Justin or Chet could answer, Micha and Eli began using paddles to pull the boat through the shallows.

"Stay where you are, catfish," Glenn said. "We're coming to you."

"'Catfish,'" Justin giggled to himself. "That's gonna stick."

"They're headed downstream, right?" Glenn asked. "How long since they were here?"

"Maybe five minutes," Justin answered. "But they're not far. I blew up their motor. They're just floating now. Wait, you already tracked them *this* far?"

"Sorta," Glenn shrugged. He was watching as his boys pulled the boat through the shallows. He was wearing polarized sunglasses that took care of the glare from the setting sun. "When we figured out the car hadn't doubled back, we bet on the river being their exit strategy? River rats, probably, prowling up and down the river. Their nest'll be upriver, betcha anything."

"And the boat?" Justin asked. He was creeping closer to the boat along the sunken timber mats, trying to meet in midway. Chet was ahead of him by several yards.

"Plenty enough, up and down here. This is actually my cousin's. He won't be needing it anymore."

*****

94

"A what?" Isherwood asked. He had heard Patrick without problem; they were only a couple feet apart from each other. He just couldn't understand it. "But why *hang* yourself? Put a bullet in your brain, at least, right?"

"Is that how you'd handle it?" Patrick asked him, raising an eyebrow.

"Well, yeah, sure," Isherwood answered quickly and just as quickly shifted the vehicle out of park. Feeling uncomfortably unsure about his response, he added, "Right?"

"I don't know," Patrick answered. "Something to think about. Or *not* think about. Should probably ask one of the priests."

"Okay, yeah," Isherwood said, thoughtfully. "But regardless, why does *this* person have a noose hanging from a flagpole? Why out in the open like that? Why not a closet or locked room or something?"

"No clue. *But,* an empty noose means we might get a chance to ask them ourselves."

Isherwood nodded as he eased the Jeep forward toward the tower. "There's something else."

"What."

"Can you see that smallish plane over there?"

"*Yeah,* was gonna ask about that. Think it could be our way out of here?" Patrick asked.

"Hey, I like it here. But no, I saw something – some*things* – moving around inside."

"You're saying we'll have to clear it out before we go to the tower?"

"Possibly. Don't know. We'll have to see how it looks first."

Isherwood drove the Jeep in an arc towards the tower, giving the plane a wide berth. He and Patrick were both watching the plane cautiously to make sure nothing suddenly erupted from it. Isherwood kept the broadside of the Jeep facing the plane, so he could use the window frame as a rifle rest, if needed. The plane seemed to wobble a bit as they passed. Something was stirring within.

"Something's weird about that plane," Patrick said. He was staring at the white plane. Two parallel lines of blue stripes swept across the fuselage. The nose of the plane was elongated and came almost to a point.

Isherwood squinted, trying to see what Patrick was seeing. Then his eyes grew wide. "Oh my God, you're *right*. It's not a plane. I mean, it is a plane, but … it's a *jet.*"

"Yeah, yeah. That's it. Can't see many of those around here, huh?"

"I don't know. Wish I knew more about all this. Think I'm about to be making that wish a lot."

"Maybe the noose person can help us there," Patrick said. "Doesn't look like anybody in there's gonna be too helpful." Then, mumbling to himself, he added, "more like, 'help' themselves to my insides."

They were nearing the tower, having passed by the jet. It was a LearJet 60 though neither man knew much about planes. Isherwood had decided to go with

Patrick's plan and was driving right up into the parking spaces beside the control building. Or, he would have had a shot not suddenly rang out.

Isherwood hadn't been driving fast, but he slammed his foot hard onto the brake. There was a short, loud screech of tires on the airstrip. It was probably a familiar sound to the airstrip, like that of a plane touching down. Isherwood cursed at himself for letting his guard down. Had he been paying closer attention, he might have seen the muzzle flash. "Did you see where he fired from?" he asked.

"Nah, no. No," Patrick stuttered. The sudden explosion of gunfire had left him rattled.

Isherwood cursed again. "He must've shot above us. Warning shot. Suppose that's a good sign."

"What?" Patrick blurted out. "A good sign? Could've ripped right through us."

"But he didn't. That's the point."

"Hold *up*," Patrick said. "The whole reason we even came here: you thought those kidnappers might've set a trap. Now, they're shooting at us, and it's a *good* thing. Sounds to me, you were right along."

"No, no. Pretty sure I was wrong about all that."

"Just because someone shot at us?"

"No, because of the gate," Isherwood began. "Also, all the zombies inside the fence. Tells me whoever's come here, post-crap hitting the fan, came from the sky. Also, that it wasn't a group or raiding party because no shot zombies. I see the effects of the initial outbreak, but nothing more. You know? Seems like somebody landed here, maybe after running out of gas, ran for cover in the tower, and trapped there ever since."

"How're you gonna say they're trapped by a half dozen zombies after they just shot at us?"

"Maybe they don't know what's going on, maybe they don't zeeks can be killed. I don't know. Maybe they're just afraid, or are trapped by something in their head. You saw the noose, didn't you?"

"So, what?" Patrick looked like a man on the verge. "We're just gonna walk right up to the building waving a white flag or something? If whatever's in there is afraid, we don't know what they're gonna do. *And*, if they don't even know how to kill a zombie, how're they gonna know *we're* not zombies?"

Isherwood shrugged. "You can stay here if you want. Might not be a bad play."

"No, if they're slow to trust, they'd *really* not trust us then."

"So what's your idea then?"

Patrick cursed.

"My idea?" A smirk was edging up the side of Isherwood's mouth.

"Whatever, jerk," Patrick sighed. "Let's just get this over with. Once more unto the breach …"

"Okay, once more," he said, pulling on the door handle.

"You leaving that?" Patrick asked, nodding at the rifle Isherwood had grabbed.

Isherwood looked down at the .22 in his hand and shrugged. "Yeah, okay." He placed the rifle across the hood of his Jeep. His sidearms, too, he unholstered and left on top of the hood. Patrick was already doing the same. "Sure hope I see little Emmy and Dee-dee again."

The men nodded to each other when they had finished emptying their personal arsenals onto the Jeep's hood. Isherwood, whether on purpose or just by habit, returned his sword to his back. They turned and began walking towards the control building. Patrick was expecting, with every step, for another shot to rip across the empty, quiet airstrip.

And then it happened. Another shot rang out.

# CHAPTER FOURTEEN:

# THE CAJUN NAVY

"There," Justin whispered. Even as he said it, the boat's motor was throttling down. Justin could feel Chet shifting anxiously in the boat behind him. His hands were audibly tightening along the rail of the boat.

Glenn nodded, "I see it." He reached back to make sure his boys were hunkering down in the boat. Both Micha and Eli were low in the boat, but still peering over the side.

Justin leveled his AR at the other boat, peering at it through the scope. It was just a shadow among other shadows drifting close to the riverbank and struggling against the swirling currents. They hadn't needed to search far for the boat. Justin had done a good thing knocking out the boat's motor, and, now with Glenn's help, they had turned the situation back in their favor.

"Dad," Eli said.

"Got it," Glenn answered without Eli needing to say another word. The boat, instead of slowing down further to approach the other boat from behind, began sweeping around it in a wide arc. Justin was confused until he began searching farther along the bank through his scope. There was another boat, a third boat. He couldn't see what it was moored onto. As before, there was no well-defined riverbank. There was only the place where the trees grew thicker. There was a scattering of trees growing deeper in the river and plenty of stumps as well. It made navigating the area treacherous, especially with all swirling water and back eddies.

Glenn looked to be trying to interpose his boat between the other two, while not getting too close to the bank.

There was soon very little point in whispering, if ever there was, given the sound of the motor. In a few moments, they were between the two boats. They were close enough to see the kidnapper's eyes now, but his eyes kept shifting away from them. Both of the girls seemed to be lying unconscious on the deck just out of sight.

Chet was the first to break the silence. He cursed at the greasy-haired kidnapper. "If you hurt her, rat fink, I'm gonna kill you."

"Look, buddy," Glenn followed up. "We've got rifles trained on you right now and another ready to blow up your new boat, just like the last time. Get out of the boat, *right now*, and we'll let you live."

The kidnapper's eyes kept shifting underneath a tangle of slick hair. He continued to say nothing, but there was an audible *click* as he cocked a pistol or shotgun that was presumably hidden across his lap.

"Classic," Justin said.

"Just shoot him," Glenn instructed. The rat boy didn't register a response, except for the constant, darting movement of his eyes.

"*No*," Chet yelled. "You could uh, uh nick the fink's brain stem or something and he might pull the trigger involuntary, you know?"

Their boat was edging closer and closer to a large whirlpool that, they now realized, stood between the rat's boat and his replacement boat. They understood too late why the kidnapper hadn't yet closed the gap to his new boat. Without a functioning motor, his boat would be helplessly trapped in the churning water and eventually capsize. Whether the rat realized it or not, he set a trap for all of them.

"Why doesn't he just give up, Dad?" Eli whispered. Glenn didn't respond but shook his head curtly, as if to say he didn't know, but for God's sake, shut up.

The tension was growing. The flickering of the rat's eyes was finally slowing. It was as though they had all grown accustomed to their rhythmic movement. They all grew uneasy at the change. Some of them even shivered, as if they had unconsciously accepted the rhythmic shifting of the eyes as a countdown of some sort.

"What the'ells he doing?" Micha asked, as he shifted uncomfortably along the slick metal floor of the boat.

The eyes suddenly stop flickering. Eli let out an audible gasp. The rat's eyes had settled on something beyond them, something in the river behind them. What happened next took everybody by surprise. Shots suddenly rang out. Small explosions, gunfire, the sound of rending metal, and water splashing broke out across the water, finally breaking the mounting tension.

******

The crack of the rifle echoed between the empty buildings of the airport and the wide open airstrip. Isherwood and Patrick both collapsed to the ground.

Isherwood called over to Patrick, but there was no answer. He scrambled over to where his friend lay.

It all seemed to be happening in slow motion. Isherwood's head and hands felt sluggish as he crawled over to Patrick. Patrick was lying still on the ground. He was looking around frantically for blood, as he crawled. There was no pool around the body. He looked back along the concrete for any kind of spray. There was nothing. He shook his friend's shoulder softly. He was limp.

"Come on, *man*," Isherwood moaned, as he rolled his friend over onto his back. He took Patrick's head in his hands and inspected it for any kind of wound. There was a bad-looking scrape on his forehead, but that was it. He patted around Patrick's chest and torso, seeing if he'd feel any kind of wet spot. Still, there was nothing. He pulled up Patrick's shirt. Still nothing.

"What the hell, man? Did'ya just faint?" He pulled on the man's limp hand and felt for a pulse. He sighed and let the arm drop back down to the concrete. He had a bottle of water in one of the cargo pockets of his pants. He spun the cap off and squeezed the bottle's contents into his friend's face. Finally, Patrick stirred as from a deep sleep. "Get up, buddy. You just knocked yourself out."

Patrick sat up suddenly and blood spilled into his right eye. He slapped a hand to his forehead and began panicking. "I've been hit, I've been hit," he kept repeating.

"Shut up, man. It's just a scrape. We'll get you a G. I. Joe band-aid out of the kit."

"Seriously? What the heck was he shooting at? Just another warning ...?" He trailed off. He was facing the Jeep and suddenly his eyes went wide. He scrambled to his feet and lunged back towards the Jeep.

Isherwood was still kneeling on the concrete beside where Patrick had been laying limp, only a moment ago. He looked back to the Jeep to see what Patrick was freaking out about. He looked to the windshield expecting to see a bullet hole there and began to chide himself inwardly for not hearing the sound of the breaking glass. But something else caught his attention out of the corner of his eye. They had left their doors open behind them, or he would have seen it much sooner. From underneath his open driver's door, he saw feet. Shambling feet. He leaned down instinctively to look under the vehicle. There were more feet. *A lot* more feet. Twenty or more.

"What the'ell you boys sittin' around for? You wanna get eaten?" It was a third voice, coming from behind them. It was then that Isherwood finally noticed the nearly headless body of a zombie lying beside the back of the Jeep. *That's where the bullet went,* he thought dumbly.

Patrick had grabbed his guns from the Jeep's hood and was already firing. He hadn't even noticed the shooter come up from behind them. The shooter was running towards them and was soon past Isherwood. For a brief moment, they exchanged glances. Isherwood was still sitting on the ground. He looked up with a pathetic expression of bewilderment on his face. The shooter looked down at him with such scorn and contempt. He was so embarrassed that he barely noticed the obvious.

"But, you're a *chick*," he said stupidly.

The woman was on about her business. She didn't even turn back to Isherwood to countenance his dumb remark. He, too, was on his feet in a flash, as if blown to his feet by the passing woman – or else trying to quickly distance himself from his embarrassment.

The woman and Patrick had both found rifle rests along the Jeep. Patrick was using the side mirror, while the woman was kneeling beside the rear bumper, as Isherwood had just minutes before.

"Try not to shoot my head off," Isherwood said as he ran past the Jeep and into the center of the advancing swarm of zombies. The setting sun flashed once more as he pulled his sword free of its scabbard. He brought the blade down across his body, slicing the cap off a long-haired woman's skull. He caught a glimpse of the jet in the distance. Another dead person was staggering through the open door of plane's fuselage. It immediately slammed down onto the hard concrete of the airstrip, five or six feet below. There were a couple more beneath the door. These were struggling towards them, unable to stand on their cracked and ruined legs. One was dragging itself forward on its elbows. Flaps of skin like shirtsleeves trailed after it. The bare bones of its elbows made a terrible grating sound as they scraped against the concrete.

Those still at the plane posed no immediate threat, and Isherwood was already swinging his blade towards the next haggard creature. They weren't dressed, he noticed, as he would've expected of people riding a private jet. He didn't dwell long on the thought, though. Just then his sword got stuck in a skull. He had struck too far below the crown, failing to anticipate the up and down movement of the zombie's lurching stride. The blade sank through the muscles connecting that half of the creature's jaw and into its eye socket. The zombie – it was another long-haired woman – looked at him with pure hatred radiating from her remaining eye. There was something familiar about that look of hatred.

This wasn't the first time Isherwood had jammed his sword, though it was happening less and less. He would typically use the sword to guide the zombie's body into a controlled fall. The body would make a slow arc to the ground, where he could plant one boot on the creature's skull for leverage. This time was different. The long-haired woman seemed fueled by a living malice. She kept advancing towards him along the edge of the blade, inadvertently shearing through what remained of her face and skull. She finished the job for him, falling into pieces just before their faces could meet.

Isherwood finished off the remaining zombies at the leading edge of the swarm. It seemed like the woman had sharpened his sword with her own skull and the sword seemed to melt through the remaining spines and skulls like a hot knife through butter. When there were no more zombies in his immediate vicinity, he began advancing on the next group. Before he could close the gap, he watched as the heads of the next two zombies dissolved into a thick red mist following the double crack of rifles firing behind him.

Not counting the zombies still dragging themselves forward on shattered legs, the swarm was soon dealt with. Isherwood hung back for a while to avoid stepping into Patrick's or the woman's firing lines. Once the rifles fell silent, though, he strode towards the crawling zombies. He would make quick work of them with his blade.

He stopped in front of the zombie with the skin flaps trailing from its elbows and placed both hands along the hilt of his blade. He noticed that, male or female, this was one of the oldest zombies he'd seen. As he was about to bring the blade down, there came a soft tap on his shoulder. He turned to see the woman's face, the shooter's face, who had not long ago looked at him with such contempt, the same look, almost, he'd seen across the face of zombie whose skull had jammed on his blade. Isherwood finally understood as he saw the tears streaking down the woman's face.

She put the barrel of her rifle into his hand. It was hot to the touch, and Isherwood quickly shifted his grasp. Without a word, she took the sword from his hand. She paused after stepping over to the zombie and bowed her head. She might even have said a quick prayer as the creature began clawing at her shoes. Then, she seemed to mimic Isherwood's stance and, after the briefest hesitation, brought the blade down expertly into the zombie's skull. Its hand stilled at her shoe. She took it and gently placed it across the chest of the elderly zombie.

# CHAPTER FIFTEEN:

# THE OTHERS

"**L**ook, Padre," Lee said, whispering. Now that the girls, or at least their unconscious but still breathing forms, were back in sight, Lee seemed to be thinking level-headedly again. It was like a switch had been flipped. "It's all just like Wilson said it would be. Don't know how the little booger knew, but he knew. Don't you see? There's a reason all of this is happening. There's a reason you just happen to have me with you. I can shoot his trigger finger off, the gun out of his lap, or the heart out of his chest, *or* all of the above. Maybe."

They had followed the odd set of images in Wilson's head to this spot, just as Justin had followed Chet only minutes before. They had even followed their own rickety path through the wooded swamp to the river's edge. Wilson had led them to the same boat that the kidnapper had stumbled upon.

They had receded back into the shadows beneath the trees when they first noticed the rat's boat approaching. They watched as the kidnapper hesitated at edge of the whirlpool. They had also watched in astonishment as Glenn's boat arrived. While Glenn, Justin, and everyone else on that boat had been focused on the rat, they watched the fourth boat creep up behind them.

"There's no time. Come on, guys. Wilson? It's gonna take all of us to fend off that last boat."

They both looked at the younger man. He was busy trying to scrape mud off his boots. When he realized they were waiting for him, he just shrugged and shook his head. Whatever had been guiding him to this point was gone now. No more visions. They were on their own.

"Do it," Padre finally said. "But don't kill him. We may need him yet. Rats always go back to their nests. Even if it ends here, it won't end here."

"Whatever you say, priest," Lee said, as he cozied up against a tree to steady his aim. He had already pulled one of his long-barreled pistols from an underarm holster. They were not far from the kidnapper's boat, maybe fifteen yards behind it. They were standing on the only high ground there was, apart from the pier that had led them to this spot.

"Get ready," Lee said.

There were several noises all at once following the pistol shot. The echoes in the wooded space made it seem like the pistol had fired several times. There were also the sounds of the bullet knocking the gun out of the rat hands and it, too, exploding. Lee had apparently aimed, perhaps unwisely, for the clip inside the gun's grip.

"Lee? What'd you do?" Padre said.

"You wanted to release him. I wanted to mark him," Lee shrugged.

"You blew the guy's whole *fore*arm off," Padre scolded.

Their conversation was quickly cut short as gunfire erupted from the fourth boat. It appeared to be full of reinforcement rats. The three men slogged through the mud towards the boat. They were holding onto the trees as the mud threatened to swallow them whole. Rat Fink, as Chet had dubbed him, had dove out of the boat and out of sight almost immediately upon seeing his ruined arm. He had slithered off just like a river rat. Padre and the others weren't worried about that just now, though. The rat's departure had edged the boat closer to the whirlpool. It would soon be out of reach.

Wilson got to the edge of the tree line and the semi-solid ground first. Lee had been slowed by the need to re-holster his gun.

When they saw Wilson, the men in Glenn's boat started cheering. Padre soon cut their cheers short with a sharp whistle. Glenn and the others responded quickly, as the priest began pointing frantically behind them. Chet didn't seem to care what was happening behind him. He was only concerned with the girls' boat as it crept towards the whirlpool. He was now leaning dangerously far over the side of the boat.

Wilson went to work fashioning a harpoon. He cut a length of vine from a tree branch above him, as high as he could reach with his spear. He then spliced his spear through one end and tied the trailing end of the vine around once for good measure. About this time, he heard the first rounds of gunfire between the two boats. This was followed soon after by a splash. He took a moment to check on the splash when he looked up to launch the improvised harpoon. It was Chet. So far, he was keeping his keeping his head above water.

"I'll be with you in a second. Just hold on, okay?" Wilson said it as though Chet were waiting for his bill at a restaurant and not drowning. "Try and keep your feet up."

While Wilson was fashioning his harpoon and tending to the women, Lee grabbed one of the rifles from Padre's back holster and took aim at the boat that was now firing on Glenn and his crew. "Watch this," he told Padre. "Like shooting womp rats back home."

Padre had no intention of watching Lee's circus act. Life was precious, *especially* these days. This is what he wanted to say, but there was no time. Instead, Padre was racing toward the boat that Rat Fink had been trying to reach. Lee had time enough for three bullseyes before he realized what Padre was up to.

"Hey, whoa," Lee said. "I'm coming, too." The boat had already started moving away from the mouldering dock, and Lee had to jump on board. Once he landed safely inside, he again took aim across the river.

Padre had to reach down into the river to grab ahold of Chet's arms. Only Chet's fingertips were still visible thrashing around at the surface. They looked like long, thin corks being dragged under. The suction was so strong, Padre was pulled headlong out of the boat. Lee had to dive to catch the priest's feet while pinning himself across the deck. The side of the boat nearly dipped beneath the waves as Padre's whole torso went under pulling on Chet. When Chet was finally pulled back over the side of the boat, they helped him get on all fours to cough up the water. Padre then turned the boat back around to where Wilson was still at work. Lee returned to shooting. Wilson, meanwhile, had managed to pull the motorless boat out of the current and to relative safety.

By the time Lee returned to the offense, he saw that the work was mostly done. After his earlier shots as well as the spirited defense from Glenn's crew, notably Justin's AR, the river rats had scurried away. They had started a wide arc to the far side of the river and were now almost headed upstream again.

Though Padre's rifles had no scopes, it was easy enough for Lee to see Glenn's boat with his sharp eyes. Something wasn't right.

"Get on, Wilson," Padre was saying. Wilson was doing his best to keep the girls' boat still while Padre moved Gill and Holly over to the new boat.

"Actually," Lee said. "Might be better for him to stay where he is."

Padre looked at Lee with scorn.

"Whoa, Padre, spare me the face. It's Glenn's boat. I think they're taking on water. You know, bullet holes and all."

Sure enough, when Padre looked in that direction, the profile of Glenn's boat appeared noticeably lower in the river. He left the bank without another word. Lee turned back to Wilson, "Hang tight, little buddy." Wilson didn't seem to mind. Being alone seemed to be his default state. He went to work retrieving his spear from his makeshift harpoon.

"Got it, Dad. It's plugged," Eli was heard saying, as Padre's boat approached.

"Good work. I think that was the worst one," Glenn answered. "Now, quick. Put this on." He had found some life vests in a cubby hole and was strapping them around everybody's chests as they worked.

"It's still too late, though," Justin said. He was holding his rifle up in one hand and, with the other, dumping water over the side with a Styrofoam ice chest.

"Doo-da-doo!" Lee mock-trumpeted. "Calvery's arrived."

"Whoa," Justin said in surprise. He had been too busy to notice the new boat's approach. "But, dude, I really hope you mean 'cavalry.'"

"Get on, boys." Glenn said sternly. "You, too, Justin. *Now*." Glenn basically tossed Eli, his youngest son, into the other boat. Justin was taking his time moving between boats, being especially careful with his rifle. Glenn shoved him the rest of the way. When Glenn finally stepped across to the other boat, it had completely submerged.

"Padre, get me back over there. I've gotta track that rat. *Quick*, before he finds whatever horse y'all rode in on."

"Wha-where it go?" Justin asked when he looked back to find the boat.

"Davy Jones locker. But I don't really know. I'm still mostly unconscious." It was *Gill*. Unbeknownst to the others, she had propped her chin up on the side of the boat to watch the transfer. Everybody turned to face her. Many of them looked as if they had seen a ghost.

"What?" She asked. "Haven't any of you seen a woman before? Holly will be along shortly, I'm sure. Get this show on the *road*. And if any of you knows what's good for you, you'll have some super-strength aspirin ready in about … five minutes ago."

"Hark, fair Juliet speaks," Justin said. They broke into laughter like the opening of a pressure relief valve. Some of them were even laughing a little too loudly, still running high from the adrenaline. They were now only beginning to realize all that they had just survived. Coming to grips with it all was still a ways off. As the last rays of the sun were disappearing one by one, it felt as if the long night was finally ending.

# CHAPTER SIXTEEN:

# AIRBORNE

By nightfall, they felt confident they had emptied the airport of any remaining zombies. Isherwood and Patrick then helped the woman arrange the bodies of her family members along the concrete not far from the jet. Padre finally broke radio silence to give them the all clear. He said they were headed by the airport on their way back to the church, if they wanted to caravan. Hearing this, Isherwood and Patrick had immediately offered to bring the woman back to the church for the night, but she had refused.

They had originally taken her for a wild and haggard woman. Now that they had got a chance to really see her, they realized just how stunning she was. She was actually on the short side, but, in her presence, they were the ones who felt short. She had long hair that would probably be blonde after she washed up. It was her eyes that really stood out, though. They were severe and piercing, but still blue enough to muddle a man's mind.

"Look," she was saying. "It's not that I don't trust you, Isherwood, either of you, really. I know you're from the church. I've been hearing you all on the radio for days now. I just need a little time, okay?"

"Brings me back to my dating days," Patrick said. "When women ask for space, give it to 'em or *else*."

"At least give us your name," Isherwood insisted. "Surely, *that's* not too much to ask?"

She raised an eyebrow at the question and didn't answer.

"Look, we're gonna bury everybody at the church, right? I'll at least learn your last name *then*." Even as it was coming out of his mouth, he regretted it. She turned on him with a flushed face, but seemed to hesitate when she saw the pitiful expression on his face.

Patrick put a hand on Isherwood's shoulder. "Come on, buddy, the lady's done enough today. We need to check on the others, anyway. You radioed in, right?"

"No," she said. "It's alright. He's right. There's no time for grieving in a world like this. It's Eve. My name is Eve."

"Really?" Isherwood laughed. Her show of trust had restored his spirits just quickly enough for him to put his foot back in his mouth. Disgusted, Patrick audibly slapped his own forehead.

"Maybe you should just go," Eve said with a voice full of hatred.

"No, I mean, it's just sort of ironic, isn't it? You're one of the last women on earth, and you just happen to bears the name of the *first* woman on earth?"

She exhaled heavily and tears were already at the corners of her eyes. When she flicked her eyes back at him, her stare was withering.

"Ouch," Patrick said. "I've seen a lot of scary stuff the last weeks, but that … dang." He had been trying to pull his buddy out of the situation. He had seen Isherwood do this kind of thing back in the day, when they were both younger and stupider, but it had been a while since he had seen his friend get in this deep. He decided to just hang back and spectate.

Isherwood cursed. He recognized that look. It was the same one he'd seen on the faces of Eve's relations, now lined up on the tarmac. "Look, I'm married. I don't mean we're gonna work together to repopulate the earth or anything. I just … ah, nevermind."

Patrick was trying to hold back, but he fell apart when Isherwood said 'repopulate.' It was actually the best thing that could have happened, because the look of fury on Eve's face melted when Patrick couldn't stop laughing. She actually joined in laughing, which only added to the look of discomfort on Isherwood's face. He had been the de facto leader of the whole group for so long. He found that he was long overdue for a dose of humility. He couldn't quite overcome his embarrassment to join in laughing, but he managed a few chirps of laughter.

"Ah, crap," Eve said when she and Patrick finally managed to contain their laughter. "I really needed that. Thank you," she said with real sincerity, slapping a hand on Isherwood's shoulder. "Yes, I think I will go back with you boys. I've been wanting to meet this priests you've got, anyway."

"Good," Isherwood said in relief. "I really didn't feel good about you being out here all by yourself."

Eve nodded. "You know," she said, thoughtfully. "I should really count myself lucky I found nice people. It doesn't sound like all groups are like yours."

"So shines a good deed in a weary world," Patrick said to himself.

"What was that?" Eve asked.

Patrick shrugged, "Nothing. It was just a line from Shakespeare. Well, also, Willy Wonka, but …"

"*Yeah*, Portia," Eve interrupted. "How far that little candle throws his beams. *Merchant of Venice.*"

"Wow," Patrick said. It was his turn now to blush.

"That 'little candle', though," Isherwood said. "That's exactly what we're planning here. Our little network of churches and forts, it's just the sort of place where civilization could *enkindle.*"

She gasped softly at the last part. She had a sudden rush of déjà vu. She felt as if she had already heard those words somewhere and was just waiting until someone came along and said them, like they were a key, somehow. "Okay," she said quietly, looking back to Isherwood. "Okay," she said again, as her voice grew stronger. "Then you've got yourself a *pilot.*"

# CHAPTER SEVENTEEN:
# AFTER HUMAN

Following the encounter on the river with Rat Fink and the rest of the Finks, as Chet dubbed them, the others all returned to the church except Glenn and Micha. Glenn had asked if either of his boys wanted to join him in tracking the rat back to his nest. Both had volunteered, though Micha was hesitant. Eli was visibly disappointed, perhaps even a little worried, when Glenn decided to bring Micha with him.

Padre and the rest left the one remaining boat with Glenn and raced back to the Humvee. "This might all still be flipped on its tail, if the rat beats us back," Padre had said.

Glenn would have radioed when he found the first set of tracks, but he figured they would soon be arriving at the Humvee. It would be just as they had left it, and they would know Rat Fink took another road.

It was a blood trail they had found. The footprints were well obscured under the water. There was at least a few inches of water covering the soft earth this close to the river. Once they found the first marker, though, the rest of the trail was easy enough to see. Cloudy patches of water where the rat had disturbed the mud were still clearly visible despite the current.

Glenn had followed hundreds of similar trails hunting deer and other large game. When they shot at a deer, they aimed for the lungs. A shot in the heart, like Cupid, would drop a deer very near the point of impact, but it would ruin large sections of the meat. A deer shot in the lungs might run hundreds of yards before bedding down to die, but all of its meat would be good. If a deer was shot in the evening, the tracking of it typically began after nightfall. So it was this night.

The blood trail of a deer shot in the lungs would be bright red. The blood was fully oxygenated in the lungs. The rat's blood was dark. The injury to his forearm was at the very periphery of his circulatory system. Also, the blood was coagulating. It didn't much matter to the trackers, though. Whether it was a splash of bright red or black, it would still look out of place to a trained eye. Regardless, the injured rat was thrashing through the swamp. He was leaving behind plenty of markers besides his blood. They anticipated hearing the rasp of his breathing or the splash of his feet anytime now.

*****

But they never did. They followed the rat's blood trail almost until the next morning. The trail finally ended in a small pool on the road beside the school. Cars had been parked tight around the school, which had once served as an evacuation point and shelter, later a bloodbath and storage for an entire swarm. The rat had apparently spotted among all the cars a model he knew how to pick easily, Glenn decided. The rat had ignored several nicer vehicles before the blood trail ended at a gap in the line of cars.

"Great," Micha said. "Now what?"

"That's only the end of the *blood* trail, son," Glenn answered. "There will be more tracks besides these."

"Never tracked anything that could drive before."

"A lot of new experiences these days," his father answered. "The roads are full of crud and debris. It'll be easy to see where a car passed."

"Ok, cool, but the roads in this area have been trampled by a few thousand feet today, *plus* that Hummer's been all over the place."

"It won't matter," Glenn said. "We know he's not going back to town or St. Mary's. There's only one other way out." He was referring to the Morganza Highway. It led northwest across the narrow land bridge that separated the oxbow river from the rest of the Mississippi River. "Trail will be easy to follow after that."

"Unless that rat's part Navajo."

"That'd be something, wouldn't it?" Glenn laughed. "They got their land back after all."

Micha's eyes grew wide and he was rubbing his hands together. "So there's just one thing left to do," he said. "Pick out my ride."

Glenn was opening his multi-tool. Micha jumped on top of the hood of the nearest car and climbed onto its roof. "There she is," the teenager smiled, pointing down the road. "And not blocked in or anything."

Micha jumped down and jogged over to a late '90s model Ford Mustang. It was a garishly-colored yellow car with purple racing stripes. Micha set about trying to pry the door open. He didn't even think about the possibility of setting off a car alarm and drawing in every remaining zombie in the area. Luckily, either there was no alarm or the battery was far gone. He threw a rock against the window, and it bounced right back at him. After finally breaking through the window, he unlocked the door and dropped himself into the black-upholstered interior. "It hasn't been *that* long," Micha said, when he saw that all the digital displays and electronics were dead. "How could the battery flat line so fast?"

"It's all this new crap," Glenn said from outside the driver's side. Micha jumped at the sound of his father's voice. "Hey, boy, you can't let people sneak up on you like that. You understand? Come on, I found something else."

At the far end of the tight jumble of cars, a flash of bright red caught Micha's eye. "Seriously?"

"Oh, yeah," Glenn nodded and then added with a wink: "Nothing like an older model."

It was scuffed and dented, but it was still held its classic lines. It was a cherry red 1964 Mustang. The interior was white leather with matching red cording. Micha swung into the driver's seat along the worn and cracking leather seats. He knocked something from bench seat as he dropped in and it clattered to the floor.

The engine was already roaring like a lion. "How'd you ...?" Micha said as his head swung between his father and the ignition. He saw his father's multi-tool sticking out of the ignition. Then he saw what he had knocked to the floor. It was the ignition cylinder. His father had already removed it.

"Thanks, but I need you to take shotgun," Glenn said as he, too, swung into the driver's seat, pushing his son over to the passenger side.

"A shotgun *would* be nice," Micha said as he pulled himself over to the far window. "We could go to that plantation where Ish and the guys found that huge stash."

"Yeah, that's not a bad idea," Glenn said as the driver's door clanged shut. Going to the Brooks Plantation would mean backtracking. "But there's another spot I've been wanting to check out," he said with a twinkle in his eye.

*****

It was a longer trip than they anticipated. Two days later, after following the course of the Mississippi River the entire time, they arrived at the outskirts of something. The tire tracks they had been following since just past St. Anne's began converging with other tracks. There were other signs of activity, as well. They backtracked a bit and hid the car in a carport inside an abandoned trailer park.

They walked along the levee, hidden beneath its crest, the rest of the way. Before long, they came to the bridge that spanned the Mississippi between Delta, Louisiana and Vicksburg, Mississippi. The Louisiana side of the river, apart from the levee, was all flat land. The topography of the far side of the river couldn't have been more different. High bluffs rose on either side of the bridge crossing. They seemed like mountains from where Glenn and Micha stood, and were likely just as defensible against zombie swarms.

Even from all the way across the river, they could see activity. It was like standing beside an anthill that a careless child had just stepped into – only these weren't ants. The bluffs were swarming with activity. Ribbons of smoke were curling skyward everywhere from little campfires. Everywhere they looked, they could see dark figures at work. They might have been digging into the bluffs, they couldn't really see for sure.

"There must be hundreds of them," Micha said in a whisper.

Glenn was just shaking his head in amazement, though he had grown pale, as well. "So *this* is the nest," he said.

# EPILOGUE

Apart from the silhouette of moonlight draped around his shoulders, the man was nearly invisible as he staggered through the darkness. His right leg had long ago stiffened. He was dressed all in black and clutched something in his left hand.

The metal rim of the old women's wheelchair suddenly stopped glistening in the moonlight, as the man's shadow fell across her frail and vulnerable body.

"Monsignor," the old woman said in a whisper.

The man in black slowed and rooted his stiffened leg like a peg. As he leaned back, the white square of his collar seemed to catch the moonlight. "I've always wondered at people our age who sleep easily," he said. "Their brains must be cleaner, the floorboards of the skull well swept, all the devils locked away in a steamer trunk at the foot of the bed."

"Skulls don't get much cleaner than yours, father," Miss Abby said.

"I suppose that's true," he said. A half smile creased his face.

"Monsignor," the old woman said again. Her tone had noticeably darkened.

"I was headed into chapel, Abby, if you wanted to join me."

"That's why I'm here. I had to take a break from that place."

Monsignor shifted heavily on his feet. He swung his arms behind his back so they were both clutching the book he was carrying. "Abby?" He asked patiently.

"There's too many people in there. It's crowded. Thems voices and faces. All comin' at me."

"It's usually empty, like before," he said.

"Not for Miss Abby," she said.

"Are there *physical* manifestations?"

*Mmm*, the old woman moaned. "They buffets agin' me. Somethin' fierce."

A sliver of a cool breeze kicked up in the night. The tops of the palm trees rattled in the night. Monsignor and Miss Abby both wrinkled their noses. Something rotten had been carried in on the breeze.

"We shouldn't talk so much out here in the open."

"Those things?" She asked pooching out her bottom lip. "They never much bothered me. I smell like death to them, mayhap."

"Just how old are you, ma'am?"

"Monsignor," she said a third time. "They're coming. You understand? They're *coming*."

"Who? *Who* is coming? Isherwood and the others?"

"Multitudes. Them's that fall on their faces. That buffets agin' me. And legion, with all the names." Tears were streaking down her face.

Monsignor nodded his divoted brow and was quiet for a time. "Which will come first?" he finally asked, but the woman just shook her head.

The *Cajun Zombie Chronicles* continue in Book
Three ...
# The Kingdom Dead

*Check it out on Amazon!*

# About the Author

Scott Smith is a Catholic author, attorney, and theologian. He and his wife Ashton are the parents of four wild-eyed children and live in their hometown of New Roads, Louisiana.

Smith is currently serving as the Chairman of the Men of the Immaculata, the Grand Knight of his local Knights of Columbus council, and a co-host of the Catholic Nerds Podcast. Smith has served as a minister and teacher far and wide: from Angola, Louisiana's maximum security prison, to the slums of Kibera, Kenya.

Smith is the author of the first pro-life horror novel, *The Seventh Word*. His other books include *Pray the Rosary with St. Pope John Paul II, The Catholic ManBook, Everything You Need to Know About Mary But Were Never Taught*, and *Blessed is He Who …* (Biographies of Blesseds).

Scott regularly contributes to his blog, "The Scott Smith Blog" at www.thescottsmithblog.com, WINNER of the 2018-2019 Fisher's Net Award for Best Catholic Blog:

Scott's other books can be found at his publisher's, Holy Water Books, website, holywaterbooks.com, as well as on Amazon.

His other books on theology and the Catholic faith include *The Catholic ManBook*, *Everything You Need to Know About Mary But Were Never Taught*, and *Blessed is He Who …* (Biographies of Blesseds). More on these below …

His fiction includes *The Seventh Word*, a pro-life horror novel, and the *Cajun Zombie Chronicles*, the Catholic version of the zombie apocalypse.

# Pray, Hope, & Don't Worry:
# Catholic Prayer Journal for Women

Scott also recently authored a series of prayer journals with his wife. *The Pray, Hope, & Don't Worry* Prayer Journal to Overcome Stress and Anxiety:

# ALL SAINTS UNIVERSITY

### EST. MMXVII

Scott has also produced courses on the Blessed Mother and Scripture for All Saints University.

Learn about the Blessed Mary from anywhere and learn to defend your mother! It includes over six hours of video plus a free copy of the next book … Enroll Now!

What You *Need* to Know About Mary
But Were Never Taught

# Pray the Rosary
# with St. John Paul II

St. John Paul II said "the Rosary is my favorite prayer." So what could possibly make praying the Rosary even better? Praying the Rosary with St. John Paul II!

This book includes a reflection from John Paul II for every mystery of the Rosary. You will find John Paul II's biblical reflections on the twenty mysteries of the Rosary that provide practical insights to help you not only understand the twenty mysteries but also live them.

St. John Paul II said "The Rosary is my favorite prayer. A marvelous prayer! Marvelous in its simplicity and its depth. In the prayer we repeat many times the words that the Virgin Mary heard from the Archangel, and from her kinswoman Elizabeth."

St. John Paul II said "the Rosary is the storehouse of countless blessings." In this new book, he will help you dig even deeper into the treasures contained within the Rosary.

You will also learn St. John Paul II's spirituality of the Rosary: "To pray the Rosary is to hand over our burdens to the merciful hearts of Christ and His mother."

"The Rosary, though clearly Marian in character, is at heart a Christ-centered prayer. It has all the depth of the gospel message in its entirety. It is an echo of the prayer of Mary, her perennial Magnificat for the work of the redemptive Incarnation which began in her virginal womb."

Take the Rosary to a whole new level with St. John Paul the Great! St. John Paul II, *pray for us!*

# Prayer Like a Warrior:
## Spiritual Combat & War Room Prayer Guide

***Don't get caught unarmed!*** Develop your Prayer Room Strategy and Battle Plan.

An invisible war rages around you. Something or someone is attacking you, unseen, unheard, yet felt throughout every aspect of your life. An army of demons under the banner of Satan has a singular focus: your destruction and that of everyone you know and love.

You need to protect your soul, your heart, your mind, your marriage, your children, your relationships, your resolve, your dreams, and your destiny.

Do you want to be a Prayer Warrior, but don't know where to start? The Devil's battle plan depends on catching you unarmed and unaware. If you're tired of being pushed around and wrecked by sin and distraction, this book is for you.

Do you feel uncomfortable speaking to God? Do you struggle with distractions in the presence of Almighty God? Praying to God may feel foreign, tedious, or like a ritual, and is He really listening? What if He never hears, never responds? This book will show you that God always listens and always answers.

In this book, you will learn how to prayer effectively no matter where you are mentally, what your needs are, or how you are feeling:

- Prayers when angry or your heart is troubled
- Prayers for fear, stress, and hopelessness
- Prayers to overcome pride, unforgiveness, and bitterness
- Prayers for rescue and shelter

Or are you looking to upgrade your prayer life? This book is for you, too. You already know that a prayer war room is a powerful weapon in spiritual warfare. Prepare for God to pour out blessings on your life.

Author, theologian, and attorney Scott L. Smith, Jr. has tested the prayers and wisdom of this book as a missionary in Africa, a minister in maximum security prisons, in the courtroom, and, most challenging of all, as a husband and father of four.

Our broken world and broken souls need the prayers and direction found in this book. Don't waste time fumbling through your prayer life. Pray more strategically when you have a War Room Battle Plan. Jesus showed His disciples how to pray and He wants to show you how to pray, too.

## Catholic Nerds Podcast

As you might have noticed, Scott is obviously well-credentialed as a nerd. Check out Scott's podcast: the Catholic Nerds Podcast on iTunes, Podbean, Google Play, and wherever good podcasts are found!

# What You Need to Know About Mary But Were Never Taught

Give a robust defense of the Blessed Mother using Scripture. Now, more than ever, every Catholic needs to learn how to defend their mother, the Blessed Mother. Because now, more than ever, the family is under attack and needs its Mother.

Discover the love story, hidden within the whole of Scripture, of the Father for his daughter, the Holy Spirit for his spouse, and the Son for his MOTHER.

This collection of essays and the All Saints University course made to accompany it will demonstrate through Scripture how the Immaculate Conception of Mary was prophesied in Genesis.

It will also show how the Virgin Mary is the New Eve, the New Ark, and the New Queen of Israel.

# The Catholic ManBook

Do you want to reach Catholic Man LEVEL: EXPERT? *The Catholic ManBook* is your handbook to achieving Sainthood, manly Sainthood. Find the following resources inside, plus many others:

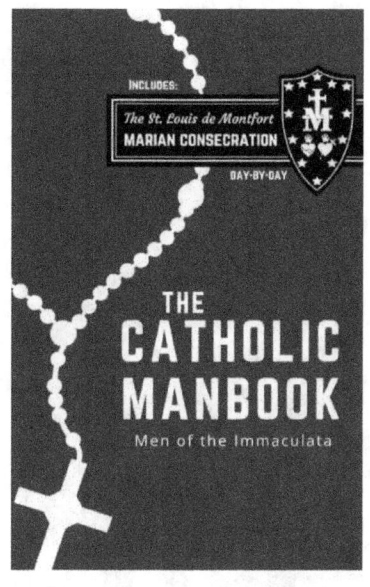

- Top Catholic Apps, Websites, and Blogs
- Everything you need to pray the Rosary
- The Most Effective Daily Prayers & Novenas, including the Emergency Novena
- Going to Confession and Eucharistic Adoration like a boss!
- Mastering the Catholic Liturgical Calendar

*The Catholic ManBook* contains the collective wisdom of The Men of the Immaculata, of saints, priests and laymen, fathers and sons, single and married. Holiness is at your fingertips. Get your copy today.

This edition also includes a revised and updated St. Louis de Montfort Marian consecration. Follow the prayers in a day-by-day format.

# The Seventh Word
## *The FIRST Pro-Life Horror Novel!*

**Pro-Life hero, Abby Johnson, called it "legit scary … I don't like reading this as night! … It was good, it was so good … it was terrifying, but good."**

The First Word came with Cain, who killed the first child of man. The Third Word was Pharaoh's instruction to the midwives. The Fifth Word was carried from Herod to Bethlehem. One of the Lost Words dwelt among the Aztecs and hungered after their children.

Evil hides behind starched white masks. The ancient Aztec demon now conducts his affairs in the sterile environment of corporate medical facilities. An insatiable hunger draws the demon to a sleepy Louisiana hamlet.

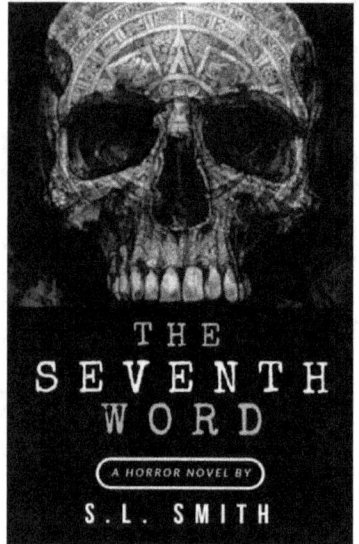

There, it contracts the services of a young attorney, Jim David, whose unborn child is the ultimate object of the demon's designs. Monsignor, a mysterious priest of unknown age and origin, labors unseen to save the soul of a small town hidden deep within Louisiana's plantation country, nearly forgotten in a bend of the Mississippi River.

You'll be gripped from start to heart-stopping finish in this page-turning thriller.

With roots in Bram Stoker's Dracula, this horror novel reads like Stephen King's classic stories of towns being slowly devoured by an unseen evil and the people who unite against it.

The book is set in southern Louisiana, an area the author brings to life with compelling detail based on his local knowledge.

# Blessed is He Who ...
# Models of Catholic Manhood

You are the average of the five people you spend the most time with, so spend more time with the Saints! Here are several men that you need to get to know whatever your age or station in life. These short biographies will give you an insight into how to live better, however you're living.

**From Kings to computer nerds**, old married couples to single teenagers, these men gave us extraordinary examples of holiness:

- Pier Giorgio Frassati & Carlo Acutis – Here are two ex-traordinary **young men**, an athlete and a computer nerd, living on either side of the 20th Century
- Two men of royal stock, Francesco II and Archduke Eu-gen, lived lives of holiness despite all the world conspir-ing against them.
- There's also the **simple husband and father**, Blessed Luigi. Though he wasn't a king, he can help all of us treat the women in our lives as queens.

*Blessed Is He Who ... Models of Catholic Manhood* explores the lives of six men who found their greatness in Christ and His Bride, the Church. In six succinct chapters, the authors, noted historian Brian J. Costello and theologian and attorney Scott L. Smith, share with you the uncommon lives of exceptional men who will one day be numbered among the Saints of Heaven, men who can bring all of us closer to sainthood.

# THANKS FOR READ-ING!

## TOTUS TUUS